# A FELLOW OF INFINITE JEST

A Luke Jones Novel

## T. B. SMITH

*TB Smith*

HELLGATE PRESS    fiction    ASHLAND, OREGON

# A FELLOW OF INFINITE JEST
©2013 T.B. SMITH

Published by Hellgate Press/Fiction
(An imprint of L&R Publishing, LLC)

Hellgate Press Fiction
PO Box 3531
Ashland, OR 97520
www.hellgatepress.com

*Editing*: Jean Jenkins

*Cover design*: L. Redding

*Author's website*: http://www.lukejonesnovels.com

Visit T.B. Smith on Facebook!

*Library of Congress Cataloging-in-Publication Data*

Smith, T. B., 1955-
A Fellow of Infinite Jest : a Luke Jones novel / T. B. Smith. -- First edition.
    pages cm
ISBN 978-1-55571-717-9
1. Police--California--San Diego--Fiction. 2. San Diego (Calif.)--Fiction. 3. Suspense fiction. I. Title.
PS3619.M5945F45 2013
813'.6--dc23
                    2013039897

Printed and bound in the United States of America
First edition 10 9 8 7 6 5 4 3 2 1

*For all those who risk mind, body and soul to keep us safe...*

OTHER BOOKS BY T.B. SMITH

*The Sticking Place: A Luke Jones Novel*

"Alas, poor Yorick! I knew him, Horatio: a fellow of infinite jest, of most excellent fancy: he hath borne me on his back a thousand times; and now, how abhorred in my imagination it is! my gorge rises at it."

*Hamlet*, Act V, scene i

Spring 1979

LUKE JONES DIDN'T WANT TO DIE OUT HERE on the street and he certainly didn't want a bunch of innocents to get splattered by a shit storm of bullets because of what he was about to do. He set the radio transmitter into the dashboard slot and waited for dispatch to confirm what he already knew about the brown Cadillac idling at the corner of Fourth and "E" Streets in San Diego's Historic Gaslamp Quarter.

A female voice responded almost immediately. "Unit 2-John, 9-7-2-Nora-Ida-Tom comes back stolen, wanted for burglarizing a gun shop and for numerous liquor store robberies. The occupants killed several LA Sheriff's deputies and wounded two civilians in a failed hot stop along the 405 freeway in Long Beach last night."

A series of three shrill tones followed. Then a simulcast over all SDPD radio frequencies started cop cars screaming in Luke's direction from across the city.

Luke eyed the occupants of the car on the other side of the one way street. A corpulent man with a crew cut overflowed the front passenger side of the Deville. Luke could see a tuft of sandy hair that narrowed into a "V" where a tattooed swastika distorted itself inside the folds of fat above the collar of the man's T-shirt. Three spiky-haired women filled the back, and a linear lean-to of a man soon sidled out the front of a liquor store headed toward the driver's seat. Smacking a pack of cigarettes against an open palm, he shifted a brown paper bag snugly into the crook of his arm, his demeanor too calm to have just committed another robbery.

Luke glanced at the ride-along next to him, a product of the Department's emphasis on community policing. A doe-eyed stunner wearing a tightly stretched T-shirt and Jordache jeans, she could have been a movie double for Jacqueline Bisset in "The Deep." But her nattering whining brought Jean Hagen's character from "Singing in the Rain" to mind instead which was enough to supersede her remarkable physical attributes.

He'd tried shutting out her grating questions and running commentary extoling him as, "... a hero for saving that other officer's life. I saw your name in the paper and got so excited when I found out you were the one I'd ride with. You do know I'm a paralegal for Gray, Cary, Ames and Frey, the largest law firm in the city? Were you on duty when the PSA plane crashed? That must have been horrible. We could see the smoke for forever that morning. We're on the nineteenth floor you know..."

The Caddy accelerated away fast, and Luke missed his chance to order her from the car. He scooted the cruiser from the curb, following at a discreet distance, waiting for the first units to arrive before initiating the stop.

Lifting his chin toward the Cadillac, he swallowed hard. "That car's full of cop killers who'll blow us away if they get the chance." Luke paused long enough to be sure she understood it was not a joke.

"Unlock your door now and open it as soon as we come to a stop."

The ride-along's breathing turned wheezy and the beginnings of an odd clicking sounded at the back of her throat. She tapped insistent fingernails against the plastic of her door. Her face turned an evanescent shade of pale as her eyes closed.

"I need you to stay calm," Luke said. "An officer will run up and use your door as cover. He'll have a shotgun and shoot anybody with a gun who comes out the passenger side of that Cadillac."

The ride-along sat still and silent except for the involuntary clicking noise.

"I'll be the one issuing orders to the people in the car. Do you understand?"

She nodded.

What he chose not to tell her was they might not have the luxury of waiting for cover units. The Caddy could pull over any second and light up the street with random gunfire from the automatic weapons stolen in the gun shop burglary.

The Nazi wannabe made a movement as if reaching under his seat and the woman behind the driver turned to glance back at the cop car. Luke hoped the bad guys believed that his horrified companion was an armed police officer. The assumption could buy them enough time for help to arrive.

# 2

THE FREEWAY ENTRANCE LOOMED A FEW BLOCKS ahead when threatening clouds released a torrent of rain. The aging squad car quivered a warning of impending engine trouble as the Caddy picked up speed toward Interstate 5. Luke willed the motor to keep going and remembered the mostly bald tires. An uncontrolled skid on wet pavement could prove deadly. If he couldn't keep up, with Tijuana only fourteen miles to the south, the skinheads might disappear into the congested traffic headed toward the border.

The engine of the cop car, a Ford Torino with a single bubble light attached, started a slow hiss as the Caddy sideswiped an El Camino, sending it hydroplaning through a red traffic signal and into the intersection of 16th and "F" Streets where it T-boned a shiny new BMW. The Caddy accelerated as the Beemer's driver leaped into the street, motioning insistently for the approaching squad car to stop.

Luke had no time to attend to traffic accidents. He veered around the gesticulating man as he told dispatch to notify Border Patrol at the international crossing in San Ysidro and to have Highway Patrol post units along the southbound freeway. If his car crapped out, some other officer would have to find the Caddy and face down the cop killers.

The woman with a hooked nose and a Woody Woodpecker hair-do who sat behind the driver turned in her seat. She had the look of a Valkyrie, especially when she folded her hand into the shape of a gun, pointed it, looked straight at Luke, pulled the trigger, and blew on her thumb.

Knowing that the murderous skinheads no longer doubted his intentions, Luke reached across the expanse between the two front seats and squeezed his passenger's cold hand in reassurance in spite of the fact he could see no light bars in his rear-view mirror and couldn't hear any blaring sirens in the distance.

The chatter of the radio soon died away, leaving him free to constantly update his location and wonder what was taking his cover unit so long to arrive. With his window open, he finally heard the low keening of sirens in the distance above the din caused by the rush hour traffic. When the first cover unit appeared in his rearview, it led a sea of cop cars undulating down the four lanes of freeway as far Luke could see.

He flipped on his overheads and announced he'd make the stop at I-5 Southbound at Crosby Street and the Deville yielded along the berm of the freeway as sedately as a family sedan pulling into a rest area for a picnic. Luke bounded from his seat as his unit came to a stop a few feet behind the suspects' car.

He sighted down the barrel of his Smith & Wesson .38 as he leaned into the space between his open door and the cab of the car. The Ford's engine shuddered into silence and steam hissed and rose through the cracks of the engine compartment as he tossed the worthless microphone onto the floor and barked out another order. "Driver, show me your hands."

Instead, the driver's door of the Caddy opened and a Doc Martens boot stepped onto the pavement as the nose of a MAC-10 automatic machine gun pushed its way into the rain. Luke knew that the bunch in the car had murdered his fellow law enforcement officers in Los Angeles just a few hours before and the terror of the moment flashed his thoughts back for an instant to his recent mandated meeting with the police psychiatrist.

# 3

LUKE ROTATED HIS WATCH. HIS BUTT HADN'T MOVED in more than an hour. He wondered if the wait constituted part of the shrink's strategy.

Less than a week before, he'd killed a suicidal gambler named Charles Henreid to save the life of his partner J.R. Shimmer. He'd had no choice even though Henreid was worth more than ten Shimmers. Shimmer was a pusillanimous little oaf who'd helped their lying and conniving sergeant shit-can Luke's best friend Denny from the police department.

Shimmer still breathed the rarified air of "America's Finest City" while Henreid cooled in a refrigerator at the morgue and Denny arrested shoplifters at the local Target discount department store. Sergeant Constantin Biletnikoff kept constant watch on the pending promotion to lieutenant he'd secured through his successful efforts to rid the Department of Denny Durango. And Luke Jones twisted in a chair as a department psychiatrist opened massive mahogany doors to extend a manicured hand.

Dr. Michele Pantages' contract with the SDPD included individual and couples counseling, psychological testing for job applicants and the mandated evaluations of officers who'd killed before they could go back to full duty. She also taught academy and in-service training classes. The contractual arrangement added up to an enormous revenue stream, but potentially compromised her doctor-patient relationships since it put her in contact with so many of her clients outside of the clinical setting.

She offered her hand and squeezed hard when he reciprocated. She'd once told him about her days as a power forward on high school and college basketball teams, a history confirmed by her athletic and graceful movements. Her short dark hair accented an elegant neck, and the abbreviated skirt she wore displayed muscular legs.

Oak paneling covered the walls of her office, the thick, rich kind that would have greeted Mycroft Holmes or Phileas Fogg in their Victorian men's clubs. Bookshelves lined two walls, and a coffeemaker sat next to a stainless steel sink. A maroon, leather loveseat faced the desk, resting next to an easy chair of the same color. Dr. Pantages clearly intended the loveseat for couples, the easy chair for individuals, and her masculine office to project gravitas to a largely male law enforcement clientele.

She'd have done her prep work on Luke during the interminable minutes since he'd handed his patient's history form to the waiting room receptionist. That information, combined with their discussions during academy class breaks, were all she'd know about him and he intended to keep it that way.

Two questions on the mostly standard questionnaire surprised him though. "Did you work the PSA 182 plane crash? If so, what was your assignment?" He knew the drill otherwise. First, she'd ask about his pre-morbid lifestyle functioning to get a baseline on his life's routines and interests before he killed Charles Henreid. Then she'd move on to the serious stuff.

"It's nice to see you again, Luke. Have a seat." Motioning toward the leather chair, she pulled her chair from behind the desk and moved it to face him.

He sat on the loveseat.

"OK, let's get to it," she said as she scratched a note on a pad. Do you have any brothers or sisters?" She tapped the clipboard holding the patient questionnaire against her thighs.

Everything Luke intended to share with her already rested in the good doctor's lap. He wasn't about to give too much away because he'd heard about the scandal created when the previous chief had pilfered psychological records during a personnel investigation. That little nugget had first cost the chief the diminishing trust of a paranoid work force then got him fired.

Bob Coleman, the current chief, had terminated the previous shrink and promised leaks wouldn't happen again. Luke trusted Coleman, but couldn't trust Dr. Pantages to protect his privacy if some future chief demanded access to his records.

Pantages tried again. "Can you tell me about your family?"

"Two older brothers and a sister. She's the oldest."

"What do they do for a living?"

Luke focused on a spot over the doctor's head, protecting himself from eye contact that might only deepen his inappropriate attraction. "My oldest brother's a preacher like my Dad. The other one's an accountant. My sister's a housewife."

"Tell me about your parents."

"Like I said, Dad's a minister. Mom died of cancer when I was nineteen, but the doctors told her she had two years to live before I was three. Pretty much all I remember about her is the process of her dying."

Pantages lifted the clipboard and scratched a quick note, probably a reminder to re-visit that loaded topic.

"Who's your favorite musician?"

Luke answered without hesitation. "Michael Franks."

"Didn't he do 'Popsicle Toes'?"

"That's him."

"Why do you like him so much?"

"He's erudite as hell and writes quirky and ironic songs with allusions to great works of art. It's fun knowing a lot of his other listeners are missing the references."

Dr. Pantages scratched another note. "Can you give me an example?"

"In 'Eggplant' he says a woman has 'a Giaconda kinda dirty look' which is a lot more clever than saying she has a wry smile, don't you think?"

Dr. Pantages scribbled another note, probably a reminder to look up Giaconda.

"Your favorite books?"

"You already know that."

"So what makes you think Shakespeare is so great?"

"Are you saying you disagree?"

"No." Dr. Pantages said it with a slight laugh. "Who's your hero?"

"Jack London."

"Why is that?"

"He declared that he wanted to live his life like a "superb meteor" and he did it while composing a library of insistent writing that described and challenged his world."

Pantages put a period to the topic before Luke could respond. "I know there are some questions about whether he drank himself to death, but we can come back to that later. What's the most fun you've ever had?"

Luke hated knowing that his answer pegged him as a guy who'd spent more time imagining a life than actually living one. "Going to plays."

He considered whether he should go ahead and state the obvious. "Watching Shakespeare, because he explores the most important aspects of being human in ways that prove those aspects are no different now than they were a long time ago. And, he doesn't just depict the good guys versus the bad guys on stage. He explores the dangerous conflicts taking place on the inside of characters like Hamlet, Lear, Leontes, Lady Macbeth and Othello, and manages to make them both more important and the same as the rest of us as he does it."

Dr. Pantages leaned forward, hurriedly scratching more notes as she spoke. "We're running out of time. But there's a lot more I'd like to talk about in the future."

His instantaneous thought—no way—must have registered on his face. An awkward moment passed before she decided to take the time for more questioning.

"What have you been doing since the shooting?"

Luke shrugged.

"Exercising?"

"No."

"Going to plays?"

"No."

"Reading?"

Luke shrugged again.

"Had a decent night's sleep?"

Silence.

Dr. Pantages pressed the issue. "Exactly what have you been doing?"

Before the shooting he'd run, worked out, read, attended plays and watched classic movies. For the past few days, he'd guzzled bourbon and beer, smoked cigars, slept almost not at all, sat on the toilet with chronic diarrhea and perched in front of the television. He'd be damned if he'd tell her that though.

He loathed this current version of himself; hated even more the notion of sharing it with a beautiful woman, and despised enduring this mandatory and intrusive process. It only increased his rage over having to kill Henreid, Denny getting screwed out of his job by a ruthlessly ambitious Sgt. Biletnikoff and his irritation with these tiresome questions. He'd be better off trying to get some sleep.

"Nothing." As Luke said it, he could almost smell the doctor's frustration mixing with the wisp of Shalimar perfume she wore. The scent reminded him of his mother.

"You were raised in a religious family. Do you ever pray for help or guidance?" Pantages asked.

"God's no help."

"Do you mean He can't help?"

"To put it in clearer language, I mean if He exists, He's toying with us."

Pantages nodded and raised an eyebrow. "How do you mean?"

Luke considered his answer carefully. "I was taking a leak the other day and smashed a crawling ant against the wall because it irritated me."

"So God's the guy at the urinal and you're the ant. Is that it?"

Luke shrugged again, knowing that his stoicism had to be driving the doctor nuts.

"Tell me about your experiences at the PSA crash."

"I'm here to talk about the shooting," Luke insisted.

"That's not all there is to talk about."

"It's why the Department made me come here."

Capitulation registered on the doctor's face as she pressed on. "So, I'm in the presence of a nihilist?" She leaned back, breathed deep and constructed a steeple with her index fingers to press against tightening pink lips.

Luke mirrored her posture, flicked a piece of lint from his pants and lowered his gaze.

Pantages dropped her fingers, straightened her skirt, nodded tentatively and leaned forward. Did she think she'd created a window of opportunity? "Tell me how you feel about killing someone."

"I don't feel anything."

"Most of my patients say they didn't have a choice in the matter. Do you feel you had any other options?"

This was suddenly getting tedious again. "I can handle it."

"I'm sensing this is hard for you, Luke. If God can't help you cope with this thing, maybe I can," Pantages said.

As she said it, Luke exploded with almost violent laughter, expelling a fragment of the rage and frustration dammed up inside him.

Dr. Pantages let loose with a cascading laughter of her own. "What I meant--what I meant was---." She hesitated thoughtfully. "Maybe you could come in for a few sessions so we can talk things through."

Pantages was stunning and formidable and Luke would have liked to see her again, but he'd be wasting time. He didn't need her help and they could never be friends now that he'd been forced to become a patient. "I don't think that's necessary." He settled back dismissively into the loveseat.

The doctor shifted tactics. "Maybe it's time to bring the Bard into the equation." She nodded toward a plaque on a bookshelf. "Do you recognize that?"

Luke had recognized the quotation the second he'd walked into her office. It was perfect for a shrink as long as the reader didn't know the full context.

> *Canst thou not minister to a mind diseas'd;*
> *Pluck from the memory a rooted sorrow;*
> *Raze out the written troubles of the brain;*
> *And with some sweet oblivious antidote;*
> *Cleanse the fraught bosom of that perilous stuff*
> *Which weighs upon the heart?*

"That's Macbeth asking a doctor to help his wife cope with guilt over King Duncan's murder," Pantages said. "Lady Macbeth's one of the most heartless characters in literature and even she needed psychological help."

Luke surveyed the office exaggeratedly before he spoke. "I see you don't have the doctor's response around here anywhere."

Pantages folded her arms and shifted in her seat. "What was that?"

"Therein the patient must minister to himself."

Dr. Pantages sighed and her body transmogrified into a question mark as her head dipped slightly and her shoulders hunched forward.

Luke thought he'd made a pretty good case for his self-reliance, but something visibly troubled the doctor. Did she think he was weak? That he couldn't handle his job? The knot at the base of his head tightened and his temples started to pound. It was a good thing she didn't know about the Professor's death or Luke's guilt over his part in getting Denny shit-canned.

Surely Pantages knew that killing somebody devastated cops more than they could possibly articulate. Luke tapped the sole of his shoe, admiring the doctor's militant tenacity in her efforts to help him. But they'd reached an impasse. "Isn't our time up?"

"It's time to book another appointment."

Luke knew the mandate—only one shrink's visit. She couldn't force him back for another appointment without documenting pathological distress. She'd have the whole police force stacked up in her waiting room if denial and unexpressed feelings constituted sufficient grounds for forced visits to the psychologist.

"OK, let's go ahead and set another appointment," he agreed, knowing he'd wait a few days then cancel it.

There were some things he wanted to say but he'd cancel the appointment anyway. He wanted to tell her he'd get stronger, not weaker, that any other outcome would be tantamount to quitting and he'd never quit anything in his life. Confronting every opponent and wrestling them into submission, that's what Luke Jones did.

"If you decide to follow through with an appointment, that would be terrific," Pantages said. "But it's imperative that you connect to your feelings. I know this all sounds like a shrink's gobbledygook to you, but it'll help--even if you like to think you don't need any help."

Luke waited silently. No way would he respond to this.

The doctor moved directly in front of him and leaned against her desk.

"Since I suspect that you're done talking to me and won't be talking to anybody else, I'm reduced to insisting that you write about your feelings. It doesn't have to be anything fancy, just an informal journal you can put into a drawer."

Luke found the familiar spot on the wall above the doctor's head as she moved toward him and offered her hand as a signal to stand. Their proximity as she clasped his hand allowed her eyes to communicate more than her mouth had had the time to say during their fifty minutes together.

Luke Jones was in trouble.

# 4

As the barrel of the MAC-10 poked into the rain, the loud whoosh of a chopper's blades repeated overhead. The rear passenger door of the Caddy opened. A woman in a red leather coat with a half-shaved head sprang out, waving a hand in the air as she dropped another hand toward her waist and shouted something that Luke could barely hear.

"Assholes!"

Luke made out "shitheads" and "pregnant" as a uniformed figure swooped past him to tackle the screaming harpy. The duo tumbled down a bank of ice plant and out of sight.

A round ratcheting into a shotgun sounded overhead. A mechanical voice rang out like God pronouncing wrath from the heavens. A deputy leaned out of ASTREA, the San Diego Sheriff's helicopter, aiming his primed weapon at the Cadillac below. The pilot thundered through his microphone. "Move another inch motherfucker and we'll blow you away."

The MAC-10 and black boot disappeared back into the Caddy.

A much closer voice spoke. "Get out of the car, honey, and run back to those other police cars." It was J.R. Shimmer at Luke's passenger door ratcheting his own shotgun round and pointing the long gun at the Cadillac. The ride-along slid out the passenger door behind Shimmer and ran for her life.

"How come no microphone?" Shimmer asked.

Luke spat out an agitated response because he knew it was his own fault for not checking the equipment before he'd left the station. "It doesn't work."

"It's OK," Shimmer said. He pulled out his handi-talkie and told dispatch to notify Sheriff's communications to have ASTREA issue the orders. "You're doing fine. Just stay calm and everything'll be OK. You're in control of this thing now."

"Driver, pay attention to every word I say." A voice bellowed from the loudspeaker above. ASTREA clearly had gotten the message to issue the orders. "Do everything I tell you to do or we will shoot you. Do you understand?"

The driver's head bounced up and down.

"Toss the gun out the window."

The automatic sailed out of the car.

"With your left hand, reach out and open the door. I expect to see the keys in your fingers as you exit."

The door opened and the skeletal driver stepped onto the asphalt.

"Now, driver, lift your hands above your head as high as you can and turn completely around until you're facing the officer behind you."

The man did as he was told. His shirt inched above his belt, exposing his midriff, proving there were no weapons hidden in his waistband.

"Driver, turn around again, but this time stop when you're facing away from the officer. Then get on your knees and cross your ankles behind you."

With the driver kneeling on the wet asphalt, ASTREA's deputies turned their attention to the fat man in the passenger seat. "You, in the front—do you have any weapons? If you do, toss them out of the car right now."

A sawed off shotgun flew out the window.

"We know there are more weapons in the car. Do exactly what I say, or we will shoot you." ASTREA's orders mirrored the ones issued to the driver. The process took a lot longer as a gigantic neo-Nazi struggled to climb out of the car and execute the turns. When he was down, ASTREA completed the same process with the two weird sisters in the backseat.

T.D. Hartson, Luke's former training officer, ran up and handed him a second set of cuffs. Luke inched forward as Hartson covered him from his left, pointing the way with a shotgun barrel as Luke holstered his gun and bent to search the kneeling suspect. He snatched the keys from around the stickman's finger, cuffed him and handed him off to Hartson who shoved the prisoner toward the cage of a police car. Another officer with a shotgun replaced Hartson. Then Luke searched and cuffed the she-dragon who'd exited from the left rear seat. Shimmer did the same with the scrawny skank and the huffing fatso on the opposite side.

Luke and Shimmer returned to the relative safety of their car doorways as ASTREA's deputies bellowed more orders. "You, in the trunk— we know you're in there. We can see the top of the trunk moving." It was a ruse they hoped would flush out any potential sandbaggers the skinheads might have secreted away to murder more cops.

Luke waited a few seconds then advanced in a crouch, doing a peek-aboo dance around the back of the Caddy, looking for anyone who might be hiding in the car as Shimmer covered him from the side. Finding no one, Luke put his fingers along the edge of the trunk and pulled up. When it didn't move, he opened it with the keys and discovered a stash of shotguns and automatic weapons, a pile of money pouches, and what looked like a couple pounds of cocaine in plastic baggies.

As he was examining the contents, a voice called out from the ice plant below. "Hey, are you guys done? I could use a hand down here. It's slippery as hell and I can't take the cuffs off my lady friend here to get her up to the top."

Luke inched down the bank a few yards and reached toward an officer with a face like a flat-iron skillet with side handles. His name tag read Bob Fiedler and Luke saw that Fiedler wore a round brass medallion pinned next to his badge with something stenciled into it. He reached out, braced his feet and pulled as Fiedler used his grasp as a fulcrum and dragged his cuffed prisoner along behind him. As they reached the top, Fiedler handed Luke the Uzi he'd wrestled from the banshee's waistband as they'd rolled in a heap down the bank of ice plant.

That's when Luke read the words on the medallion. "I Got Ugly." He'd definitely have to ask about that when he got the chance, but he first had to figure out what to do with his ride-along now that the rest of the shift would be taken up with report writing and impounds.

Shimmer was way ahead of him. He volunteered to let her ride with him for the rest of the shift.

# 5

ON A DAY OFF, LUKE PARKED HIS AGING MERCURY TRACER near La Jolla Cove as the sun's nadir dipped beneath the horizon line and initiated a spectacular rose and gold sunset. He grabbed the coffee he'd picked up at the Girard Avenue Pannikin where he saw Dr. Seuss and his wife Audrey Geisel sharing a patio table with Jonas Salk and Francoise Gilot. Nestling into an enclave of rocks, he pulled out a notebook and pen. He scanned the waves rolling toward the La Jolla Shores Hotel then twisted around to look up the cliffs at the rear of the buildings on Prospect Street.

L. Frank Baum had started his heroine Trot's adventures from this cove location in The Sea Fairies, part of his Wizard of Oz Series, and Raymond Chandler had once frequented the Whaling Bar in the La Valencia Hotel at the top of the cliffs. What could Luke possibly write to stand up to those literary heavyweights?

Screw it. He wasn't there to write literature and nobody would see what he put on paper anyway. He'd probably never bother reading the stuff again himself.

The nearby bark of a sea lion pulled his attention back to the ocean where a mini-cascade of wavelets licked the shore and pushed outward again. The water created an incessant whooshing sound, a reminder of the blades of the Sheriff's copter that had saved his life. He took a deep

breath and wrote by the glow of his powerful police Kel-Light a highly
weather and shock-resistant flashlight constructed of heavy "aircraft
aluminum" which made it perfect for night police patrol and for use at
the beach.

*I've decided to follow Dr. Pantages' advice and start a journal to see if
it'll help me sleep. I just wish I'd brought a cigar to defend myself against the
stinking gull and seal guano that's surrounding me on the rocks.*

*What was it Macbeth had said about sleep? That it "knits up the ravell'd
sleave of care...balm of hurt minds, great nature's second course, chief nour-
isher in life's feast."*

*I can't remember what real sleep feels like since I see the headless torso of
the suicide victim from my first radio call when I close my eyes. Or I watch
my slow motion bullets slamming into Henreid's body before seeing him
crumple against the cold concrete of the Golden West Laundromat. And I see
the Professor's lifeless body propped against the wall and wonder what I could
have done to save his life. Sure, he was a depraved drunk, but he had more
insight into what made me tick than any sober preacher I've ever met. I wish
I could talk to him now to get his take on this mess I'm making of my life.*

*Sometimes as I'm nodding off, I see what I saw and I smell what I smelled
at the PSA crash. That's when my eyes shoot open and I crawl out of bed to
pour another shot of scotch or bourbon. But I've got to stop that. I don't want
to end up like the Professor.*

*Right now, I'm sitting in the middle of a twisted metaphor for my life
as darkness blankets the ocean, masking its undulating abyss and blocking
any sight of the natural beauty that's all around. Since that nasty stink is
creeping up my nostrils, I've decided to write about the plane crash.*

*Chicken Little's prediction came true on September 25, 1978, when a
Boeing 727 collided with a Cessna 172 and the planes crashed to the earth
near the corner of Dwight and Nile Streets in the North Park neighborhood
of San Diego. I was in my final field training phase then, but my training
officer had decided I could work a one man unit while he worked another
car, shadowing some of my calls to make sure I didn't screw anything up.*

*I was drawing a diagram on a traffic accident report when a citizen pointed out a nose-diving jetliner with its right wing aflame and black engine smoke spewing into the blue sky behind it. I got in my car and followed the vertical column of smoke that trailed from the earth up into the sky and arrived at the crash site less than ten minutes later.*

*Literary critics say you can read an entire Hemingway novel without finding any reference to smells. I don't know how he managed to become such a genius while leaving details like that out of his work. The stink of the searing magnesium, flaming grass, plastic plane seats, furniture, stucco, charred flesh and hair and blood sucked all the oxygen from the air. The Santa Ana winds, hot off the desert, pushed waves of heat at me that scorched my cheeks as I stepped from the car. When the dry smoke stung my eyes and sent a stream of tears rolling along my cheeks I understood why some people chose to call what I was experiencing Devil Winds.*

*There seems to be a spot in the brain where a smell stays forever once it's crawled up your nostrils and taken a seat beyond the sinuses. I smell that smell every day now. Dad told me he still smells it four decades after leaving the U.S.S.* Nevada *to man a skiff searching for survivors from the U.S.S.* Arizona *at Pearl Harbor.*

*No words can describe the stink of that day and there's no possible way to forget it.*

*What surprised me most as I stepped out of the car was seeing that a TV news crew had beaten me to the scene. Then I saw an academy classmate, Hank Hunter, and remembered the station had been following him for a special profile since our first day of class. The cameraman stood behind him as he stared toward the edge of the horizon and crouched next to a sizzling torso in the gutter. From the cameraman's angle, he couldn't record the furling and unfurling pages of a partially scorched novel that whipped around Hunter's ankles, but he did catch the action as a page flapped against his chest and blew away in the wind. J.R. Shimmer, Hunter's fifth phase training officer, stood next to him, looking mesmerized by the flaming torso. I guarantee none of us had ever seen anything like this before.*

*I'm tempted to compare what I saw and smelled that day to a battle scene from a Shakespearean play, but the Bard can ultimately only depict puny people acting words out on a stage. Hunter's labored breathing hit my gut hard. I saw a helpless expression behind his tears as he wiped stinging soot away from his eyes. He'd been my main rival in the academy and, as far as I knew, everything in his life had come easily to him before he tore his rotator cuff breaking up a double play at second base. His father, a Black Cuban, had risen from illiterate refugee to become the superintendent of a large Florida school district and his Hispanic Dominican mother had been the principal of the high school he'd graduated from as class valedictorian.*

*He'd spent half a season as a San Diego Padre and ripped his shoulder to shreds in front of the home crowd, so his entrance into the academy about a year later made him a local cult hero. Seizing the opportunity, the department offered him to the media as an example of its increasing diversity and transition to community policing. He disappointed nobody since he beat me out for honor graduate and won the physical fitness award as the unqualified star of the academy.*

*I could lift heavier weights and crank out more push-ups, but he sailed through the obstacle course as easily as I can step on to a curb from the gutter and he ran the four-forty in near world class time. He was as athletic as Mickey Mantle and as graceful as Fred Astaire and people instantly liked him. That's a skill I'd like to emulate some day.*

*I followed Hunter's gaze to a spot on the ground as he inched forward to stand over two hands that were clutched together. The one with thick fingers wore a wide wedding band. The second, feminine hand displayed flaming red nail polish and a large diamond set in a platinum ring. Both arms were severed at the elbows.*

*I touched Hunter's arm to let him know I was there and the absent resolve returned to his eyes as he reached a finger to flick away ashes settling on his sweaty cheeks beneath his eyes. He was the public face of the SDPD and the television crew was about to see what I now saw: a high-functioning hero. We stood together for a couple minutes, two rookies on the cusp of police careers, surveying the devastation.*

*A splayed pair of shoeless legs jutted from the windshield of a BMW. Across the street, half the body of a uniformed stewardess had skewered the roof of a Volvo.*

*A sobbing woman hurried up to lead us to a nearby house where blood was dripping on her couch from the ceiling and a living room television displayed pictures from the camera crew outside. We did what we could to console her and I told her the kind of help she needed would be coming later. I had no idea how long it would take. I walked to the edge of the crater in the asphalt. What were we supposed to do?*

*Hunter pointed out the complete lack of traffic noise. No dogs barked and no birds sang. "Listen to the silence," he said, "and look at the people walking around but don't focus on their bodies. Look at their faces. You can see whose souls are obliterated."*

*I coughed and gagged from the smoke that had built up in my lungs and bent to spit a gob of phlegm onto the sidewalk. That's when I saw Sgt. Biletnikoff walking up and putting his hand on Shimmer's shoulder.*

*I later learned that 144 people died in the planes and on the ground. None of the bodies I saw that day had any faces. And the faces of the living people looked dead.*

# 6

SERGEANT BILETNIKOFF SAUNTERED INTO THE LINE-UP ROOM, ran his comb through his thick moustache one last time and shoved it into his pocket. Although he was in his early thirties, with his baby face, he could have passed for a teenager. He shoved a hank of fine sandy hair away from his forehead and started calling out the beat assignments, assigning Luke to work unit 2-John, the one-officer car in the center of downtown San Diego. It was the beat that contained Horton Plaza, anus of the earth, and much of the historic Gaslamp Quarter, a sixteen-block district slated for extensive redevelopment efforts along with the funds to do the work and tax incentives necessary to attract wealthy investors.

Instead of using common sense observations by seasoned supervisors, department policy dictated that one and two-officer beat cars were determined by a complex formula measuring the average number of minutes officers were out of service on radio calls and arrests during their 480 minute shifts. Sometimes extra cars were assigned to specific beats and supervisors occasionally partnered officers together if manpower allowed and the officers agreed to team up.

Shimmer spoke up as soon as Biletnikoff called out the last assignment. "Hey, Sarge, how about letting me and Luke work together tonight?"

The room fell silent. Every officer in the room knew of the animosity between Luke and Shimmer except for Bob Fiedler who'd just transferred onto the squad from Southeastern Division under a cloud of rumor. But that animosity had its roots from before Luke had saved Shimmer's life, and Shimmer evidently intended to make nice from now on.

The black circles under Shimmer's eyes were obvious. Luke figured the little guy, who looked like he could easily play one of Shakespeare's lowlife characters from the history plays, wanted a rookie partner to do all the work so he could sleepwalk through his shift. Hell would drip with pointy icicles before Luke would let that happen.

"That sounds good to me." Biletnikoff grinned as he said it, letting Luke know he couldn't care less about the opinion of a big-mouthed newbie and didn't intend to ask for his input. He also apparently loved the idea of sticking it to the rookie a little since several officers had singled Luke out for special recognition the night he returned to full duty after the Henreid shooting. Too many Luke Jones love-fests had to roil the ulcer juices in Biletnikoff's gut.

"There's not much to report in the incident log down here, but the Sheriff's Office had a weird 261 at the beach in Encinitas last night," Biletnikoff said. "I got to tell you, this suspect is messed up. He made the victim tie her boyfriend up with a rope and raped the girl in front of him.

"There's not much by way of description. He's about six-foot and wiry, so he's probably one-seventy to one-ninety, somewhere in that range. He wore gloves and a ski mask and basically blinded his victims with a flashlight before brandishing a gun to prove that he meant business. He didn't say anything other than ordering the woman to tie the guy up."

Biletnikoff shifted behind the lectern for a second and Bob Fiedler took advantage of the momentary silence. "Hey Sarge, aren't you going to say anything about Luke's hot stop?"

Biletnikoff glared. "I thought Jones could talk about that when we go around the table. He was fortunate spotting that car."

Luke knew this was as good a time as any to keep his mouth shut. He would have too, if it were anybody but Biletnikoff. Sometimes he just couldn't help himself. "Luck is what happens when preparation meets opportunity," he said.

"Cripes, Jones, can't we get through one lousy line-up without you quoting Shakespeare?" Patches of skin reddened along the sides of Biletnikoff's neck.

"Seneca," Luke answered.

"What?"

"Lucius Annaeus Seneca said it, not William Shakespeare."

"Yeah, Sarge," Shimmer chimed in. "That Seneca guy said it, not Shakespeare."

T.D. Hartson walked in before Biletnikoff could respond. He wore a blue business suit and was accompanied by Sgt. Caroline Rood, President of the Police Officers' Association, who could easily look down on the top of his white hair as she strolled in behind him.

"Excuse me, Sgt. Biletnikoff," Rood said. "Could I take just a moment to make a quick announcement?"

"Of course," Biletnikoff said, apparently glad for the chance to quit talking about the hot stop.

All gazes riveted on Rood who strode to the podium. She had a perfect alabaster complexion, short flaxen hair, and wore an elegantly tailored linen suit. Her accumulated successes in a man's world clearly aided her command of the room. She sparkled with confidence as she nodded toward Biletnikoff.

"Thanks for letting me take a couple minutes. I just got out of a meeting with Chief Coleman who's asked me to make an announcement." She motioned for Hartson to join her at the lectern.

"I'd like to introduce you to Sergeant T.D. Hartson," Rood said. "The Chief just gave him his new badge, and he'll be leaving us for northern division starting the day after tomorrow."

The sounds of applause exploded throughout the room and officers near Hartson reached out to shake his hand while a few standing nearby punched his shoulder and others offered high-fives. Pretty much everybody's eyes in the room were on Hartson, but not Luke's.

Biletnikoff instantly paled, looking like somebody had just clobbered him upside the head with a pole axe. He caught Rood's eye and stammered out a question.

"Excuse me, Caroline. What do you mean leaving 'us'?" She was President of the Police Officers' Association, not a member of Central Division.

"I'm sorry. I guess I should have explained that a little better. As of today, I'm your new lieutenant." The announcement brought a brief hush to the room until Fiedler started a round of applause for the first female lieutenant in the history of the San Diego Police Department.

Luke kept his gaze riveted on Biletnikoff who took a half-step backward and almost stumbled over a chair. The man had clearly expected to receive the lieutenant's promotion after he'd sucked up to Deputy Chief Browner and lied on the official police supervisor's report that forced Denny Durango to resign from the Department.

Whether Lt. Rood noticed it or not, she made no indication. She extended her hand to the flabbergasted sergeant. "I'll see you tomorrow night at the One-Five-Three Club for the promotional celebration." She looked directly into her new subordinate's eyes to communicate that the statement constituted an implied order. "It'll be great having you work for me," she said.

She held Biletnikoff's gaze for a long second then turned in Luke's direction. "Before I go though, I'd like Officer Jones to tell me about his hot stop. I hear it was a great piece of work."

Luke was better at challenging bloviating authority figures than he was at tooting his own horn. His hesitation allowed Shimmer to jump to his feet and tell the story in great detail, omitting the part about Luke's forgetting to inspect his microphone at the station before his shift started.

"Like I started to say," Biletnikoff interjected, "Jones was fortunate to be at the right place at the--"

"Nah, Sarge," Fiedler interrupted. "Officer Jones here spotted the cop-killing scroats from LA after a quick glance at the Investigative Supplemental. Did any of the rest of you guys see that at line-up that day?" He looked around the room to a nearly universal round of head shaking. "He not only nailed the whole gang, he got 'em with a boatload of weapons, drugs and cash. What exactly did you recover in that car, Luke?"

"I'm sure communications is stacking calls..." Biletnikoff said.

"I read the report," Fiedler said. "There were forty-two guns, about twenty grand in cash and close to a pound-and-a-half of coke. Not bad for an officer's first hot stop." Fiedler hung his hands in the air for a second then started clapping and almost everyone in the room joined in.

Biletnikoff clearly had a brand new pain in his ass. "OK, enough on that," he said as he pointed at the golden medallion on Fiedler's shirt. "That 'I Got Ugly' thing's not an authorized part of the uniform and I want it gone."

"Actually," Fiedler said. "The Chief gave me special permission to wear it for a year."

"Nonsense."

"It's true," Lt. Rood offered. "I heard the Chief say it when he attended Southeastern line-up to witness Officer Fiedler getting a CO's citation for the Ugly arrest."

Luke loved seeing Biletnikoff stymied on all fronts.

The sergeant stomped toward the door and stopped in front of Fiedler as officers gathered around Rood and Hartson to offer their congratulations. "That bitch you tackled at the hot stop wanted to file an excessive force complaint against you," he told Fiedler. "She claims she's pregnant and may lose the baby on account of you. I don't have time to waste investigating a bullshit complaint like that but you broke every safety rule in the book exposing yourself to danger the way you did out there."

Luke couldn't believe what he was hearing.

"You've obviously got a Godfather looking out for you somewhere up the chain," Biletnikoff continued. "So there's nothing I'll be able to do about that right now, but you better watch your ass from now on."

Luke sidled up to put his two cents worth into the conversation before Biletnikoff could disappear into the sergeant's office. "Hey, Sarge, have you considered writing a commendation for Officer Fiedler here because of all the lives he saved out at the hot stop? That woman he tackled was reaching for an Uzi you know, and what he did probably stopped her from lighting the freeway up with gunfire. I put it in the report. You did see that, didn't you?"

Biletnikoff's face approached the color of cranberry sauce and the color ran down his splotchy neck and under his uniform shirt.

"Guess not," Luke said as his face took on a grin to rival the one Biletnikoff had worn when he'd assigned Luke to work with Shimmer. "Try not to get too down on yourself about the promotion. Something good'll come your way one of these days. You know, Shakespeare said setbacks can be good for you. How did that go exactly? Oh yeah, 'sweet are the uses of adversity,' that's what he said."

Biletnikoff's response sounded like a round of shots fired at the pistol range. "Are you stupid or something? There's nothing sweet about adversity."

"It's an oxymoron," Luke said over his shoulder as he went to offer congratulations to his two new superiors.

# 7

DEPUTY CHIEF HAL BROWNER STOMPED INTO Chief Bob Coleman's
outer office to find the inner door closed and Donna Walker, the
Chief's stone cold fox of a secretary sitting at her desk. Browner knew
she was fiercely protective of her boss, and he was thoroughly pissed
that her current loyalty belonged to Coleman and not to him.

"Can I help you, Chief?" Donna asked.

Browner was pretty sure Donna knew of the animosity between
him and Coleman, but hoped she'd respond to his sense of indignation
and help him out even if she sensed his intention to make more trouble
than usual. Yes, he was a deputy chief and not the Chief, but he wasn't
about to let Coleman stomp all over him.

"I need to see him. Is he in?" Browner said.

"Lieutenant Rood is in with him right now."

Browner inched toward the closed door, hoping that the sense of
urgency his movements conveyed would encourage her to interrupt the
meeting.

"I'll tell him you came by as soon as she comes out," Donna said.

Browner shifted his weight from one foot to the other several times
then reached for a banana in his jacket pocket and started unpeeling it.
Like most executives on the SDPD, Browner grazed like a rabbit and
spent either the early morning or his lunch hour jogging along the em-
barcadero past the coast guard station a couple miles on toward Lind-
bergh Field and Shelter Island.

Chief Coleman, a heavy smoker, defied the rule for being in shape that usually precipitated an advance into the highest ranks of the police department. But that didn't make him a rule breaker. He was the first Jewish chief of a major police department, and claimed that his Jewishness helped him understand what it was like to be a social outsider. He'd skyrocketed through the ranks by attending volatile meetings fomented by militant factions of the city's minority communities, claiming he did it to re-build the bridges destroyed by the riots of the sixties. Browner was sure that was bullshit, that he'd done it strictly to curry the favor of community types who had the nerve to believe they should have a say in who the city manager appointed to the top position. One of the first things Coleman did once he became chief was to appoint a Hispanic and a Black detective to function as full time liaisons to the minority groups from which they'd emerged. It added up to a waste of manpower as far as Browner was concerned.

"You don't want me to interrupt?" Donna asked. It was too late for the question. If she was really willing to do that, she'd have taken Browner's first hint. The phony question thoroughly pissed him off since it put Donna squarely in Coleman's camp. She'd come up with some lame excuse not to follow through with his request if he pressed the issue.

"How long has she been in there?"

"I'd guess about ten minutes or so."

"Was this a scheduled meeting?"

"She came in and asked to see him after she announced the sergeant's promotion at Central line-up. Is everything OK?"

This was about enough to send Browner over the edge. Donna had to know that the promotion pronouncement at line-up before the official department-wide announcement was not the way to do things. He stood and steamed for a few seconds. "Does he have anything scheduled following the meeting?"

Browner leaned close to sniff the honeysuckle essence of Donna's chestnut hair as she flipped through the calendar on her desk. "He's got a meeting with the editorial boards of the San Diego Union and Tribune at two, but nothing before then."

Browner shuffled backwards to the outer door. "I need to see him. Have him call me as soon as he's done?" He couldn't help making his request sound like an implied order and wondered if the wrinkle at the corner of her mouth was an involuntary smile or a sign of irritation.

"I'll ask him," Donna said. "Is there anything else?"

"No. Just have him call me right away," Browner said.

Lt. Rood walked out a couple minutes after Browner had exited the outer office. Chief Coleman followed close behind.

Donna Walker related her conversation with Deputy Chief Browner as soon as the new lieutenant left the area.

"I'm going to lunch," Coleman said. "Wait ten minutes, then call and tell him I've gone. I'll be going to meet with the editorial bunch over at the Copley building after that. Let him know he can see me in my office at four o'clock if he wants to."

"Today's Tuesday. He's got a standing meeting with the downtown Lion's club at 4:00." Donna said. "And tomorrow you're tied up all morning with the Mayor."

Coleman grinned, the white of his teeth a stark contrast to his dark hair. "I hadn't thought of that," he said as he left through a puff of smoke.

# 8

"UNIT 2-KING AND 3-JOHN TO COVER, we're getting a third call about the occupants of a white Toyota Corolla pelting pedestrians with water balloons." The dispatcher assigned the call to the two officer unit with Luke and Shimmer and assigned Paul Devree to cover. "The first incident occurred at 3rd and Ivy. The second at First and Broadway and this third one's coming in from the Palace pawnshop at 900 Fifth Avenue."

Devree pulled his unit to the curb in front of the pawnshop in time to see a disheveled drunk shuffling down the sidewalk toward "E" Street. His hair and coat were soaked and his shoulders heaved as he sobbed.

Jim, the pawnshop's owner, greeted Devree at the door. Well known to the downtown patrol officers because two women who worked for him dated officers they'd met at the shop, Jim was a reputed straight shooter who ran a classy business in an industry populated by shady characters and shabby storefronts.

"Hey, Paul," Jim said. "Three teenagers in a white Toyota just pulled to the curb and started pelting that homeless guy with water balloons. They threw the balloons as hard as they could and cackled the whole time until he sat down in the middle of the sidewalk and started to cry. He took off when you pulled up. Probably figured he'd get arrested for something."

"You get a plate?"

"They pulled away about the time I figured out what was going on. You won't have any trouble spotting them though. They had one of those Jack in the Box heads on their antenna and the radio was blasting hard rock."

"The victim's GOA," Devree told dispatch. "Do we have any word about either of the other victims?"

"I'm getting a request for an ambulance at 3rd and Ivy that's probably related. I've dispatched Unit 4 Henry to make the transport to Centre City Hospital. Hopefully, they can get a better description from the victim."

Devree provided Luke and Shimmer with the vehicle description and asked that they check the area while making sure they understood that he wanted to be the one to take the report.

The dispatcher soon advised that all the victims appeared to be homeless which was something that Devree had already figured out.

The volume of radio calls heated up as Luke drove a north-south grid on the numbered streets between Market Street and Broadway and he soon volunteered to break off of the water balloon call to handle an armed robbery in front of the Pickwick Hotel on lower Broadway. An armed robbery obviously had to take precedence over a call involving a couple of kids tossing water balloons.

The anger in Devree's voice shot through his radio transmission. "3-John, tell 2-King negative on that. I've located the victim from Fifth Avenue. He's got welts all over his face and neck and his chest is starting to hurt. He has a history of heart disease. I'm carrying this case as a 245."

Luke was about to snatch up the microphone in protest, but Shimmer immediately intervened to calm him down. "There's a reason Devree won't let this thing go," he said. "It's best that we trust his judgment.

"Who ever heard of a water balloon attack as an assault with a deadly weapon?" Luke answered.

"Do you think Devree is a chicken-shit cop?" Shimmer asked.

"I know he's a straight shooter," Luke answered.

"Then trust his judgment and do as he says," Shimmer said.

Luke hated to admit it but Shimmer made perfect sense.

"Devree clearly wants the three punks in the Corolla in custody, so let's stick with it and help him get that done," Shimmer said.

Luke soon heard music blasting from a white Corolla a few cars ahead of them on Sixth Avenue and asked Shimmer to light up the overheads. The request was their first sign of détente and the beginning of a real partnership.

"Unit 2-King," Luke said. "Advise 3-John that we've got the Corolla stopped on Sixth just north of Broadway. Can he bring the victim by for a curbstone line-up?"

"That's negative at this time," Devree said. "I'll need an 11-41 at my location. The victim's got pain in his jaw that's starting to run down into to his left shoulder."

The dispatcher asked Devree several questions to be sure she had sufficient information to relay and dispatched the police ambulance crew from the adjoining group of beats to the scene.

Devree rounded the corner onto Sixth Avenue several minutes later and pulled in behind the other police car that partially blocked the east lane. He immediately stomped to the Corolla, jerked the driver out by the collar and ordered the two others to step onto the sidewalk.

The trio of teenage miscreants wore blue high school letterman's jackets from Crawford High School with water polo insignias on them. They shifted their feet tentatively and exchanged a couple of timid glances. The effect must have been the opposite of how they almost certainly appeared when they prowled their high school campus hallways as mini-masters of their school universe. "I need you three punks to stand there on the corner and not move. Is that clear?" Devree said.

The trio nodded a semi-defiant recognition of the order, but kept elbowing one another and laughing to drum up the courage to stand up for their God-given rights. They all stood about six-foot and carried themselves with an insistent swagger that advertised a cultivated sense of entitlement.

Devree selected the driver as his focal point and stared him down until the youth relinquished his bravado and lowered his gaze to look at the sidewalk. That's when Devree opened the rear door to the Corolla and exposed a couple dozen water balloons on the backseat. He asked if there were any more balloons in the trunk and demanded the keys when he got no answer.

"My Dad's an attorney," the driver said, "and I know you don't have the right to search anything."

"Does Daddy know what an asshole you are?" Devree fired back.

"You can't talk to me like that," the boy said. The other two, clearly followers, chimed approval of their leader's defiance.

"I said, give me the keys, and I'm not going to ask again."

The driver reached into his pocket and handed Devree the keys.

"Why are you doing this?" Devree demanded.

"Doing what?" the driver responded.

Devree turned to Luke who stood about half a head taller than anyone gathered on the sidewalk. "Did you have any trouble understanding my question, Officer Jones?"

"It was pretty clear to me," Luke said. "Wasn't it clear to you Officer Shimmer?"

"It was perfectly clear to me," Shimmer responded.

The driver finally gave up the ruse. "Nobody cares about these guys. They're stupid bums who my Dad says are a drag on society."

A muscle in Devree's neck twitched as he unlocked the trunk. It was full of water balloons. He left the trunk open and told Luke and Shimmer to keep their eyes on the boys as he walked to the cab of the car. He leaned in several times and carried the remaining water balloons to the trunk. With his arms bent to carry the load, his biceps bulged beneath the short sleeve of his shirt. His after-shift workouts were definitely paying off.

"He doesn't really intend on charging them with ADW?" Luke asked Shimmer. He was as pissed as Devree but was almost certain the charge wouldn't fly.

Devree overheard the question. "I guess that depends on what we find out from the hospital," he said as he turned to the boys and ordered them to stand still.

"We can move around if we want to," the driver insisted.

"OK, then." Devree walked back to the car, put the key in the ignition and lowered the two closed windows. "Since you want to move so bad, get back in the car," he said.

The boys' expressions suddenly showed open fear and uncertainty about how to behave in the face of such flagrant abuse. It convinced Luke that no one had ever demanded anything difficult of the boys in their entire lives. The expression around Devree's eyes also clearly communicated his unwillingness to tolerate any more defiance from these teenaged boys who clearly thought it was OK for them to abuse anyone not from their station in life.

Devree almost growled as he took a step toward the driver and the teenagers immediately piled into the car. Devree pulled several water balloons from the trunk and started throwing them one by one at the mortified boys who sat helpless in the car.

"Ow, that hurts. Stop that," the driver said. Then, each time one of the boys was blasted with an exploding water balloon they cried out with pain and with anger.

But Devree repeated the process until the last balloon was spent.

"My Dad's gonna have your job," the driver insisted through jags of tears. He tried to force himself to stop crying and gulped out his next words. "You can't get away with doing this to us."

"Get away with what?" Devree demanded. "You don't see anything wrong with what just happened, do you?"

The three teens clearly thought there was something wrong with somebody pelting them with water balloons while they sat helpless in the car.

"I'm willing to swear that you three punks got so excited from your little spree that you had a spontaneous water balloon fight," Devree said.

Words were interspersed with sobs. "That's not what happened and you know it," the driver insisted. "You'll never get away with this once I tell my Dad."

"Go ahead and tell your Daddy," Devree said. "It's worth it even if it does cost me my job. But it won't. We might be coming to arrest you after we hear from the officers with the victims at the hospitals."

"Hospitals?" the driver said. "We didn't hurt anybody!"

"How would you know dummy? You didn't stop to see if your victims were OK. Either way, I'll swear that you and your friends are full of shit and I'm pretty sure my partners here will back me up."

Shimmer and Luke both nodded in affirmation.

"There's more than one type of justice," Devree muttered as he walked past his squad mates and piled into his car.

# 9

"UNIT 2-KING, DID YOU EVER GET A UNIT TO HANDLE THAT 211?" Luke asked dispatch a few minutes later.

"Affirmative, 2-King, 5-John is handling the 11-10, but I could use a unit to check the area for the suspects."

"Go ahead with the description."

"Suspects are two white males, well over six foot and more than two hundred and fifty pounds, wearing cowboy boots and hats. The weapon was a knife with about a twelve inch blade," the dispatcher said.

"Ten-four, anything on the loss yet?" Luke asked.

"Unit 5-John?" the dispatcher asked.

"It's starting to look like a drug deal gone bad," Unit 5-John said. "I'll advise further in a few minutes."

Luke acknowledged the information and he and Shimmer started their search. With the rodeo in town for an event at the Sports Arena, it suddenly seemed like about every third person on the sidewalk was wearing cowboy boots and a hat and had a knife sheathed on their belts. But most of them were not nearly as large as the description provided by dispatch. It took several minutes before the officers saw tandem cowboys who stood about equal to Luke's height and weighed more than his two hundred-twenty pounds.

Unsure of how effective Shimmer would be as a cover officer under the circumstances, Luke asked for another unit before pulling to the curb and contacting the cowboys whose hats towered over the rest of the people walking along the sidewalk.

"Excuse me, gentlemen," Luke said. "I need to see some ID."

"What's the problem officer," the taller of the two men asked.

A police cruiser pulled to a stop near Luke, and Officer Dick Arenas stepped into the street. Luke nodded a signal of appreciation for the cover as he cautiously approached the cowboys. "I'm checking out a report of a robbery, and you two gentlemen have the misfortune of fitting the suspects' description. I just need a few minutes and you can probably be on your way."

Both men pulled out wallets that were secured to their belts by a chain, from their rear pockets.

Luke moved forward. "I'll have to take those knives, too, so you don't cut me all to pieces," Luke said with a smile. He tossed them onto the driver's seat of his police cruiser, then put up the windows and locked the doors.

"You can have them back when you leave. You don't have any other weapons do you? Hand grenades, bazookas, anything like that?"

Both men chuckled as the three men assessed one another and the instant psychic rapport common among physical giants gelled.

Luke utilized the standard field interview stance, standing about three feet from the closest cowboy with his left hip and leg slightly in front, keeping his gun out of their reach. "I'll need you to stand over there by my partner and put your hands on the hood of my car." Luke nodded toward the man farthest from him who instantly did as he was told.

"Unit 2-King," Luke said to dispatch. "Do we have any more about the loss in this 211?"

"Unit 5-John, any additional on the loss?"

"Unit 5-John, this is turning into a hold-pending," the other unit responded, indicating that the report wouldn't be assigned a case number and that the victim was most likely lying about the robbery. "Just have the officers cut a couple FIs on the two he's got detained and we can let the detectives sort this out."

Luke patted both cowboys down, checking for any more weapons as Shimmer wrote down their physical descriptions, identifying numbers, phone numbers and home addresses in the central California ranch country. He also included where they were staying while in town and all the information needed to complete the field interview slips for submission to the robbery detectives. Then Luke gave them their knives back and sent them on their way.

Luke thanked Arenas for the cover and started for the car.

"Don't thank me," Arenas said. He'd recently transferred on to Biletnikoff's squad from another watch.

"Why's that?" Luke asked.

"I've heard a lot of shit about you," Arenas said. "You're a punk who needs to keep his mouth shut and never call for cover on this type of bullshit again. You've already got a partner and besides, real cops got better things to do with their time than babysit you."

"What are you talking about?" Luke asked. He'd never heard such unmitigated nonsense in his life.

"You and Shimmer have guns and those two assholes only had knives. You don't need cover to handle something like that when there are two of you. And now that I know what a chicken shit you are, I'll never come when you call for cover again."

Arenas was dead wrong. A smart cop always had plenty of cover when contacting potential armed robbery suspects. Luke started to take a long step toward Arenas but checked himself. He always got in trouble for spouting off, and the last thing he needed was to engage in open conflict with another uniformed officer in the public eye. He needed to learn to keep his mouth shut sometimes and now was a good time to start. He and Shimmer got in the car, and Luke caught a glimpse of

Arenas' face in the rear-view as he drove away. Arenas had him pegged for a blow hard who'd back down when a better man challenged him and Arenas clearly thought of himself as a better man. Luke filed the knowledge away.

# 10

HAL BROWNER PUSHED BOB COLEMAN'S OFFICE DOOR closed behind him the next afternoon and stood glaring at his boss. He'd hoped Coleman would open his mouth first, but the asshole just sat there staring at him, refusing to fire the first shots in what was sure to be an angry dialogue. What a power player this guy thought he was.

Browner finally ended the pregnant silence. "I demand to know why you pulled those shenanigans with the lieutenant's promotion," Browner said.

"I'm not sure what you mean," Coleman answered. He took a fresh Marlboro from the pack and fired up, incensing Browner, who knew Coleman smoked in front of him just to piss him off. He'd gotten the word that Coleman secretly referred to him as a granola eater and an earth muffin.

"I'm in charge of field operations and I intended to promote Biletnikoff," Browner said. "It should be my call and you know it. Then, to top it off, you had Rood announce her promotion to the guys at Central Division a full day before you put out the department announcement."

Coleman puffed and blew. "What's your point?" He asked the question with that irritating half smirk that always made Browner's cheeks get hot.

"You made the promotion after I sent out word that I'd made my choice. Then you sent that woman over to Central Division to announce your decision just to make me look bad."

"I'm at a loss here," Coleman said. "Just how did that make you look bad? You didn't tell anyone of your selection without telling me who it was, did you?"

Browner plopped into a seat.

"Do you want to know what I think?" Coleman kept right on talking without waiting for an answer. "I think you intended to promote Sgt. Biletnikoff because he helped you exaggerate the truth to get rid of that Durango kid."

"I don't know what you're talking about."

"You know exactly what I'm talking about. Durango embarrassed the Department with that arrest at the "America's Finest City Rally" a while ago, and you retaliated by having Biletnikoff go after him."

Coleman blew a line of smoke rings in Browner's direction. "It really pisses me off that I didn't find out in time to do anything about Durango. You know I won't tolerate any form of retaliation against my officers. Yet, you had your lackey Biletnikoff drum up false charges against him to force him to resign and put you in good stead with Mayor Pillson and Councilman Cleveland."

"That's nonsense," Browner protested. "You're using that as an excuse to promote Rood to make points with the community over promoting the bitch to lieutenant."

"Don't ever talk like that about one of our female employees," Coleman said.

"You've been looking for an excuse to promote the first woman to middle management for a long time now, and I told you we don't have anybody ready yet. But that didn't stop you did it?"

"Look," Coleman said. "I'm not going to debate you about who deserves the promotion. You'd better get clear on the fact that I run this department."

"Are you saying you're taking over patrol operations?"

"Only if I have to," Coleman answered. "I won't tolerate mistreatment of any of my employees and I'll tell you this much, you better not screw with Caroline Rood. I'll have your ass if word gets back that you're mistreating her because she told me what you and Biletnikoff were up to."

Bang. Coleman tossed a hot grenade with that pronouncement. Nobody had said anything about Rood's role in the Durango affair, and it was the first Browner had heard of it.

Chief Coleman glared for a long second. What he said next made it clear he'd told Browner about Rood's participation in the Durango affair for a purpose. "You and that bunch over at Southeast tried firing Fiedler over some penny ante violation of the rules and regulations in that Ugly thing. He deserved a commendation but you wanted to get rid of him just because he'd won his job back fair and square through a civil service appeal. And that firing was over a bunch of trumped-up bullshit as well. That's the end of it. Are you 10-4 on that?"

"That guy has no business in an SDPD uniform." Browner shot back.

"Let's be clear on something," Coleman said. "Don't ever fuck with any of my people for personal reasons again." Coleman let the message sink in. "In case it's not clear to you yet, everyone who works for this department is one of my people."

# 11

THE ONE-FIVE-THREE CLUB BUSTLED BIG TIME BY the time Luke stepped in. Owned and operated by a police department mechanic, the shabby bar took its name from a police form with a dubious reputation for the role it often played in police misconduct investigations.

Most of the personnel from Central Division not actively patrolling the streets or having to get up early for morning shift had come to celebrate Hartson's promotion to sergeant and to welcome the new lieutenant to the division. Luke pushed his way through to the bar, sizing up the crowd along the way.

About half of his patrol squad surrounded the pool table. It was mostly the group that had accepted him in spite of his odd insistence on quoting the Bard and constantly comparing his experiences to something he'd read. They appreciated his physical prowess and mental toughness and shared his antipathy toward Biletnikoff, mostly because of the sergeant's willingness to stab anybody in the back to get ahead. Luke had an extra reason for hating Biletnikoff, his tacit support of senior officers who enjoyed hazing rookies.

"Nine-John Randolph," the inveterate stutterer who worked Unit One-John and took about nine tries to spit his call sign out stood chalking the end of a pool cue. It was a signal that he'd won the previous game and was ready for any challenger with a quarter in his pocket.

Frances Patrick Eugene "Francie" O'Brien, a devilishly funny raconteur who Luke and Hartson knew to be a coward, occupied his normal position near the center of the group. According to the rumor mill, he'd applied to several police departments and would be leaving soon.

A loud chorus of voices sang out above the zoinking and clanging of the pinball machines in the back room. Luke had seen them gathering in the back and knew they were comprised of several of Biletnikoff's favorite officers. They shared their boss's belief that rookies like children, should be seen and not heard. And the actions that belief generated had put Luke in direct conflict with most of them at one time or another.

Lt. Caroline Rood dominated a group of women huddled by the window. Andee Bradford, Luke's academy classmate, stood closest to the bar. She'd taken her jacket off and exposed her uniform pants. And the white cotton T-shirt that was usually covered by her uniform shirt turned her chest into a magnet that pulled male eyes down and away from her face. Luke respected the way she stood up for herself when mistreated by male counterparts and admired her courage with the crooks on the streets. Several female patrol officers and detectives, most of whom Luke didn't know, filled out the remainder of the group.

As Luke leaned over the bar to get the bartender's attention, Bob Fiedler settled in next to him. "I know you're new," Fiedler said. "Have you gotten any feedback on the hot stop?"

Fiedler bought two Coronas and slid one in front of Luke.

"I looked for you the other day to talk about it, but couldn't find you. I guess it doesn't matter. I'm sure Sgt. Biletnikoff covered it by now or maybe Hartson. I heard he was one of your training officers."

Luke swigged his beer, "No one's given me any feedback. I haven't had a chance to talk to Hartson yet, and don't go making the mistake of thinking Biletnikoff's actually interested in acting like my supervisor. He hates my guts. Vice versa, I might add."

Fiedler took a sip and nodded. "He hates me too."

"What's his beef with you?"

"Field Ops forced my transfer on him."

Luke shrugged and sipped and decided not to wait for Fiedler to ask the same question of him. "I'm told I have a teeny bit of trouble keeping my yap shut sometimes." His eyebrows arched, trying to signal that he was a master of the art of understatement at the moment. "I keep hearing rumblings about some kind of cloud hanging over your head. What's that all about?" Luke asked.

"My sergeant over at Southeast Division got pissed when the Department assigned me to his squad after the Civil Service Commission reinstated me from a termination. He's been dogging my ass ever since and tried firing me again when I arrested the guy in the Big Ugly series. But he couldn't get away with it because my lieutenant wrote up a commendation instead. I went to the POA about the way I got treated and the next thing I knew, I got transferred to Central working for Biletnikoff. Now, he hates me as much as my other sergeant does. These guys can be a pretty unforgiving bunch."

"Why were you fired in the first place?" This nugget about fighting for your job through the Civil Service Commission was uncharted territory for Luke. Maybe Fiedler could coach him up on how to get Denny's job back.

"It's a long story. I'll tell you about it some time," Fiedler said.

"What's this Big Ugly thing all about? And how come the Chief gave you special permission to wear the medallion?"

"Where's Luke Jones!" Shimmer shouted from near the pool table. Hank Hunter, who'd been trained by both Hartson and Shimmer and now worked at Northern Division on the squad that would soon report to Hartson, stood nearby. A trim woman with a Padre's cap on stood between Shimmer and Hartson. A couple inches taller than both men, she stood with her hand lightly touching Hartson's arm. "Meet my wife, Beverly" Shimmer shouted to Luke. To his wife he said, "That's Luke Jones." Then he started a hullaballoo of encouragements for Luke to quote a little Shakespeare in honor of Hartson's promotion.

That clinched it. Luke would have to accept that his relationship with Shimmer was forever changed since he'd saved the little guy's life. Too bad it didn't happen before Shimmer had helped Biletnikoff eighty-six Denny from the Department.

Determined not to set himself apart from the crowd, Luke shook his head and asked for another beer. But Shimmer's shouting got more insistent, leading a chorus of increasingly boisterous voices as several guys started pushing Luke toward the pool table in the center of the room. "A toast to Sergeant Hartson!"

"Hell, yeah," Hartson insisted. "A little Shakespeare to celebrate my promotion."

Luke looked around stalling for time to think of the best quotation for the occasion. As several people pushed and nudged him toward the table, a hand reached out to grab his bicep and the woman who suddenly stood next to him stepped to her tip-toes and kissed him on the cheek. It was his ride-along from the other night. "Shimmer invited me," she said. "I hope you don't mind."

"I don't mind," Luke said, and gently pulled his arm away.

Ride-Along says, "I'd like to buy you a beer when we get a chance." But Luke's answer got swallowed up in the noise as the crowd kept pushing and jerking on him, and more and more people called out for a Shakespeare performance.

"There's really nothing in Shakespeare apropos of celebrating a police promotion." Luke made the pronouncement with a grin, knowing his word choice would be more than even Hartson could stand.

"Ditch the big-word bullshit and just give us some Shakespeare, for once?" Shimmer shouted.

Luke climbed on top of the pool table and his mind raced through Shakespeare's canon, coming up empty on the topic of a promotion. "I can't think of anything that fits the occasion," he said.

Dick Arenas' voice boomed from the back room. "Finally, Luke

Jones at a loss for words. It's about time he kept his mouth shut for a change."

The bombastic pronouncement was all the motivation Luke needed to take advantage of his superior position on top of the pool table. "At least now I have the perfect citation for the occasion," he said. "But, first, would all you guys in front mind forming a little circle here in front of me."

Arenas bellowed from the back room as the animated group formed the circle. "Some of us are sick of your bullshit, Luke."

Luke had expected Arenas to assert himself after he'd pegged Luke as a punk during their encounter with the rodeo cowboys. "I can't see you guys in the back," Luke said as a set of hands started waving in the air and Hunter mouthed the silent words, "don't do anything" in Luke's direction. Hunter was the master of restraint, but it wasn't a skill that Luke shared.

"I can certainly appreciate your sentiment," Luke yelled. "Tell you what, I'll shut up and get down from here if you guys will humor me for just a minute."

The vanguard of the gang in the backroom shuffled to the doorway between the two rooms with Arenas leading the way.

"Ducdame, ducdame, ducdame!" Luke glared openly at Arenas as he shouted over the heads of the officers who'd formed the circle in front of him.

"Duck what?" Arenas shouted. He perpetually leaned forward when he walked. With his thick neck, pug nose and odd swinging gait, it gave him the appearance of a hyena's weird amalgamation of canine and feline characteristics and lent the impression of an animal that couldn't be trusted.

Luke lowered the volume of his voice. "Ducdame. Ducdame."

Arenas snatched at the bait. "We can't hear you."

Luke cleared his throat. "I think I'm losing my voice. Can you get a little closer, so I don't have to shout?" He looked down at the group that had formed the circle. "Would you guy's mind making room for Officer Arenas and his friends? Let them get real close so I don't have to raise my voice."

Luke motioned for Arenas and his entourage to move forward.

"What was it you said a minute ago?" Arenas asked as his group walked inside the circle.

"It wasn't important," Luke said.

"Bullshit," Arenas insisted. "What does that duck thing mean?"

"Oh, you mean ducdame," Luke said.

"That was it. What does it mean?"

Luke had set Arenas up and decided to clobber him with full chapter and verse. "I don't really know. But, according to Shakespeare in Act two, scene five of *As You Like It*, it's an invocation to call fools into a circle."

# 12

THE SERGEANT'S OFFICE WAS AS QUIET AS THE DALAI LAMA'S house after somebody swatted a fly when Devree slipped in after his workout. Exercising at the end of the day had its advantages. It helped him unwind before joining the gang at the One-Five-Three Club and let him reconnoiter the joint in case anything interesting was left lying around.

He'd picked the habit up a few months before after finding something in the homicide office that really embarrassed the department once he sent it to the papers. He hadn't intended to embarrass the Chief back then, but wanted to stick it to the creeps who were going after Luke's pal Denny. The creeps turned out to be Deputy Chief Browner and his minion Constantin Biletnikoff. The publicity worked too, except Biletnikoff had outmaneuvered everybody by lying on a supervisor's investigation report and trumping up charges against Denny relating to something that happened a little later on. Not even Devree could have imagined that a police supervisor would lie on official police reports to ingratiate his way into a lieutenant's promotion.

Shit like that was just flat wrong. Devree felt like sometimes it was his job to make things right, even if nobody knew what he was up to. And it wasn't always necessary to get in somebody's face to gain an advantage. He believed a cop's job was to protect the weak and the innocent from the aggressive and the manipulative. It was too darn bad

Luke Jones couldn't learn you don't always have to confront your ene-
mies head on to get the job done.

A thud sounded in the lieutenant's office like somebody banging
against a metal file cabinet. Then Devree heard footsteps followed by
another thud, then more footsteps, and what sounded like a bookcase
toppling over. How could he not go and investigate?

He heard some thunking noises behind the closed door, twisted the
handle and pushed it open a couple inches. A sliver of light crept in
from the hallway highlighting a blonde guy wearing a Hawaiian shirt,
flip flops and Bermuda shorts. There was just enough light to show that
Biletnikoff was the asshole climbing up on the lieutenant's desk. What
the hell was he doing up there?

Devree got the answer as soon as he heard the sound of trickling
water and saw an arc of liquid shoot out from beneath Biletnikoff's
shorts. The sonofabitch was pissing on the lieutenant's paperwork.

Biletnikoff had done some mighty weird things since the PSA
crash, but how could he not bother to make sure nobody was around
before he turned his piss gun on Lt. Rood's shit? Devree eased the
door closed and headed for the sergeant's office.

He sat at Biletnikoff's desk and scratched out a note on an interof-
fice memo. "I saw you pissing on the LT's desk. No telling when I might
use that little scoop to your disadvantage." He picked the top drawer's
lock with a letter opener to slip in the note and saw a legal sized envelope with some photos inside. They were the ones Luke had told him
about that displayed a naked Tina Cleveland, chief of staff for, and
daughter to, the powerful city councilman. Belitnikoff and Browner
had catered to the councilman by getting rid of Denny Durango who'd
snapped the pictures.

Luke had told Devree that Biletnikoff used the photos as a trump
card when it came time to force Denny to resign. Man, would it bust
Biletnikoff's chops when he saw they were gone. He snatched the envelope, closed the drawer and headed to the locker room to dress and

get the hell out of there before Biletnikoff came back. Devree's post workout shower would have to wait.

He pushed his way into the One-Five-Three a few minutes later, just in time to see Lt. Rood pushing Arenas toward the door with a stern order to get out. What the fuck was happening to this place?

He ordered a bourbon and soda and a beer for Sgt. Hartson, deciding not to tell anyone about Biletnikoff for the time being. If it was true that knowledge was power, he was one powerful sonofabitch right about now. Biletnikoff walked through the front door and sat beside him smelling of booze already and the edges of his eyes were bloodshot. He'd obviously already stopped at the One-Five-Three Club when Devree was working out. He handed Biletnikoff Hartson's beer.

"Hey Sarge," he said. "You look like you could use a drink."

# 13

ARENAS SWIGGED THE LAST OF HIS BEER AND STOMPED OUT of the Club as soon as Lt. Rood let go of his arm. She'd had to step in to keep Arenas from trying to pull Luke down from the table.

Luke caught a glimpse of Devree who'd just slipped through the door and was surprised to see him buying Biletnikoff a beer. "There is a little something from Henry the Fifth that seems appropriate for celebrating Hartson's promotion," he said. "But, I have to improvise a bit."

The room quieted as Luke spoke.

> In peace there's nothing so becomes a man
> As modest stillness and humility:
> But when the blast of war blows in our ears,
> Then imitate the action of the tiger:
> Stiffen the sinews, summon up the blood,
> Then lend the eye a terrible aspect;
> Now set the teeth, and stretch the nostril wide,
> Hold hard the breath, and bend up every spirit
> To his full height!

Luke hoisted his Corona. "And follow T.D. Hartson into battle! Here's to a humble mentor when times are quiet, a steady hand when things get tense, and a kick ass warrior when the shit hits the fan."

Shimmer kept his bottle hoisted after everyone shouted approval and took a drink. "That same shit can be said of Luke Jones!" he shouted. "Here's to the man who saved my life!"

A quieter round of shouts followed from about half the crowd and Luke started to climb down from the table. But Shimmer wouldn't hear of it. "Give us a little more Shakespeare before you get down," he insisted.

"I think that's enough," Luke said.

"Come on Luke," Shimmer tipped his bottle in the ride-along's direction and gave a little wink. "That was great, but doesn't that guy ever say anything the ladies might like?"

Andee Bradford seemed to like the idea and egged Luke on. "Give us a little something about love," she said.

"Yes," one of the other women insisted. "How about a little of that stuff from *Romeo and Juliet*?"

Feeling more than a little full of himself, Luke turned his gaze on the ride-along who stood staring up at him in rapture. He edged forward and commanded her eyes with his.

It is my lady. Oh, it is my love
Oh, that she knew she were!
She speaks, yet she says nothing. What of that?
Her eye discourses. I will answer it—
I am too bold. 'Tis not to me she speaks.
Two of the fairest stars in all the heaven
Having some business, do entreat her eyes
To twinkle in their spheres till they return.
What if her eyes were there, they in her head?
The brightness of her cheek would shame those stars
As daylight doth a lamp…

Several of the women whistled as Andee Bradford repeatedly shouted "Encore," and let loose with a series of construction worker whistles. "Give the lady some more."

Never losing eye contact with the ride-along, Luke thought for a second and quoted something from the second part of *Henry the Fourth* as he slowly ran his gaze down her body and back up again.

I faith, sweetheart, methinks now you are in an excellent good temperalilty:
Your pulsidge beats as extraordinarily as heart would desire;
and your color I warrant you, is as red as any rose...

The ride-along offered her hand to help Luke descend from the bar. She was a stunner and really seemed to appreciate the Shakespeare stuff. As she pulled him toward the door, Luke decided there might be more to her than met the ear.

# 14

LUKE WOKE UP ALONE THE NEXT MORNING AFTER his first decent night's sleep in weeks to find a sealed note on the pillow next to him. He'd shower and drink some coffee. Then he'd open the envelope and savor last night's memories.

The shower spray soaked in an odd sense of relief as Luke soaped his body. Maybe all he'd needed was love, or a little sex, or maybe both. If that turned out to be the case he could forget about keeping that stupid journal.

After he dried and dressed he pulled a record from its jacket and put Michael Franks on the stereo. Joe Sample's crisp piano filled the room, followed by a high-pitched voice letting loose with some of Luke's favorite lyrics. "We touched, like watercolour fawns, in landscapes painted by Cezanne, like lovers floating painted by Chagall..."

Luke stepped on the seeds Denny's parrot was constantly dropping all over the kitchen linoleum. At least his roomie had shown enough sense to cover the cage before going to bed. Luke took his coffee to the balcony overlooking the pool, savored a sip, and opened the note.

*"Dear Luke, You are so gorgeous lying there as you sleep. What a body! I didn't have the heart to wake you. Had to get home to my drip of a fiancé. You're a hero and I'd love to see you again. It's best if you call me at work. Shimmer has the number. PS, You were amazing last night!!!"*

Luke read the note over a couple times before wadding it up. She'd never mentioned a boyfriend, let alone a fiancé. What had happened to the concept of trust in relationships? How could she betray her fiancé like that and still have the nerve to want to see the guy she cheated with again? Luke's stomach twisted and his head pounded. Sure, he knew they hadn't stood a chance as a couple. But he had certainly never intended to participate in a betrayal.

He didn't regret the sex. The sex was great, but he'd been screwed another way too because she'd made him her unwitting accomplice. They'd only had the one night, but that didn't mean he shouldn't be able to trust her not to use him.

He closed his eyes, missing the feel, smell and taste of her, seeing her dark hair draped over her naked shoulder as she straddled him. She'd turned out to be nice and even intelligent once she stopped gushing all that crap about him being a hero. Even her voice got mellower and more modulated once that happened. And she had sounded elegant as hell when she moaned and called his name.

Luke sipped his coffee and gazed out on what had been a sparkling morning a few minutes before.

Then he picked up his journal and wrote.

*You wake up in the morning*
*from a night of what should have been love*
*and dream*
*in chiarascuro fragmentations*
*what you would have painted*
*if you'd only had control of the brush*
*and a song comes on the radio*
*asking*
*who can I turn to?*
*but you can't answer*
*because*
*who can you turn to*
*when you can no longer look to yourself?*

# 15

DENNY NUDGED HIS LATEST DISCO CONQUEST OUT THE front before opening the balcony door. He was a mixture of Hispanic and Black blood which showed up, not only in his appearance, but in his mixture of affectations and his face looked a lot like the mouse that gets its kicks scooting into a hole a whisker ahead of the cat's paw.

As it turned out, his expression was joy, not relief. "I saw somebody slipping out of your room last night," he said. It almost sounded as if he was singing.

Luke took another sip of coffee.

"Is this a great morning or what?" Denny said.

"It's OK."

"OK? It's freakin' fantastic. You can't tell me gettin' a little sumpin' at night don't make getting up in the morning a whole lot better."

Luke shrugged and sipped his coffee in silence, his expression a message that Denny was full of shit yet again.

"Come on, Luke" Denny said. "You're a good looking guy. You ought to put a little more effort into gettin' some every day the way I do.

Luke raised his eyebrows.

"What?"

"Nothing," Luke said.

"You should get some more strange ass for yourself," Denny said.

"You already look like a new man since last night."

"One's about all I can handle."

"So, you'll be seeing this one again?" Denny asked. "What's her name?"

"I don't think so."

"You don't think what?"

"That I'll be seeing her again."

"Why not?"

Luke handed Denny the note which sent his roomie howling with laughter.

"Are you kidding me?" Denny said. "This is perfect. Just line up a few more and your love life'll be as good as gold. Let's you and me go to the disco tonight and get you started off right."

"I work tonight."

"Only till eleven-thirty. We could get to Crystal T's Emporium by twelve-fifteen and be back here by two with a couple pieces of ass in tow."

Luke shook his head. "Not tonight."

"You've been saying that same shit for months now. If you don't want to go out, why don't you call that babe from last night and have her waiting here when you get home?"

Luke gave his roomie the middle finger salute and headed to the kitchen for another cup of coffee.

"Be that way but quit worrying about me," Denny said.

"You don't have time to be having too much fun. You should be focusing on getting hired by the Sheriff's Office not on getting laid," Luke insisted.

This was no longer friendly banter.

"Just how dense are you?"

Denny fired him a look which indicated the conversation was over.

Ending the conversation may have been Denny's aim but that didn't mean Luke had to cooperate.

"Don't you care anything about love?"

"My mama loves me," Denny said. "That covers the love part. Everything else is about gettin' some. You can't tell me that getting some of that fine ass strange like you got last night isn't better than the work it takes to fall in love."

Luke couldn't help but grin.

"What did you say your girl's name was?"

Luke looked at the dregs of his coffee. "Ride-along," he said.

# 16

ALTA CALIFORNIA'S REPUTATION AS PARADISE STARTED WITH a mythic fantasy penned by Sixteenth century Spanish poet Garcia Ordonez De Montalvo. Although he'd never seen North America, Montalvo wrote of "a mysterious place of uncommon beauty and unparalleled wealth… with rivers full of gold that emptied…into the sea from the interior," and called the place California.

About thirty years later, a Spaniard who'd helped Hernando Cortez to conquer the Aztec Empire, saw the real California when he captained an expedition of three ships into the waters past what's now known as Point Loma into "a very good enclosed port." Juan Rodriguez Cabrillo named the waters the Bay of San Miguel after one of his ships.

Despite the grand notions conjured by Montalvo's poem, the sea captain and his crews soon sailed northward without finding any treasure. Sixty years after their departure another seafaring Spaniard, Sebastian Vizcaino, took over the naming rights. When Vizcaino re-discovered the inlet, he called the waters "The Bay of San Diego."

In modern times, San Diego's seventy miles of beaches and bay shores annually lure tsunamis of tourists seeking respite from the thrumming pressures of workaday lives in other parts of the country. Many decide to stay permanently and go home only long enough to pack their belongings and return to the Promised Land.

San Diego's waters hide such marine dangers as man-eating sharks, seasonal storms and deadly undertows powerful enough to pull a person underwater before spitting the body back toward the land. But those dangers are created by nature, as predictable as the tides, and not at all mysterious.

It's the dangers lurking on the land that boggle the mind.

A ski-masked man with a flashlight in his jacket pocket, a rope in his hand, and a six-shooter in his waistband wondered how two people could be stupid enough to be embracing under the cliffs at Torrey Pines beach just below the fabled golf course when the freaking news was full of reports of the "maniac" rapist who made women tie their man's hands and compelled him to watch the woman being raped. Was it possible these morons didn't know no one was out here protecting them at two o'clock in the morning?

OK. So tonight's weather was beautiful and its blue moon cast an opalescent light along the sand, making it tough for a predator to hide in the shadows. Still, if the couple rubbing crotches and nestling in the rocks thought their choice of coarse terrain would keep them safe it was a sad mistake. Didn't these dummies know that summer lured people to the beach, which enticed a committed rapist to strike, exactly the way the San Diego Union and Tribune newspapers had written about three times already?

They were about to get what they deserved and it'd really be nice if he could tell these people how dumb they were. Unfortunately, he had to keep his mouth shut. No sense giving the dummies a way to identify him through his voice. Not that he expected to ever be in a lineup, voice, visual or otherwise.

He pulled the flashlight from his pocket and flashed its beam into the guy's eyes. And the dumb shit complained and put his hand in front of his face--like the light was the worst problem in his stupid life that night. Then the rapist pointed the flashlight at his gun to prove he was in charge before handing the girl the rope and pushing her at her man.

He loved the way the woman's hands trembled as she fumbled with the rope. She was scared shitless and her worthless man didn't have the guts to try and stop what was happening. The poor bastard was powerless, which was exactly what the rapist expected to see.

He motioned for the guy to scrunch to his knees and started unzipping his own Levis. Even then, the guy groveling in the sand was too stupid to figure things out. The woman's "protector" actually offered him money to go away and leave them alone. Lame move. He wasn't there for money. These dumb-shits were about to get exactly what they deserved and all they'd get from him by way of reciprocation would be a couple grunts when he shot his wad.

The woman knew the score. She sobbed and wailed like a hungry baby. These bitches immediately knew what he wanted and he always wanted the same thing, his dick inside them. The women knew he intended to fuck them because they wanted to get fucked. That much was sure. But the guys were always too stupid to figure things out until it was too late.

He reached for her and she unbuttoned her pants. Hell, she even put it in for him when he slapped her. She was something to look at now that most of her clothes were stretched out on the sand. He'd known she would be. All these late-night beach bitches were. He kept his mask and shirt on and pulled his trousers down part way. They couldn't identify him if they didn't see too much.

It was all getting too easy.

He hoped she appreciated what he was doing for her, proving what a coward her man was so she didn't need to spend the rest of her life figuring it out. All he had to do was keep his gun trained on the cowering punk and he could do whatever he wanted to the woman.

He grabbed the girl by her hips and snuggled her to him, deciding he wouldn't hit her again if she was good. She quivered with pleasure as he pushed his way deeper inside.

Then she started sobbing. Ah, no crying man! Crying totally pissed him off. What was so horrible? It wasn't like this was her first time.

He backhanded her, told her to shut up and her sobs backed off, sounding more like disgusting burps and hiccups. It was almost enough to interfere with his rhythm.

He covered her mouth. Ah, yeah. Much better now. He hit her again. It had to make the guy feel like shit, watching his bitch getting slapped and fucked. He'd go easier on her if she didn't pretend so hard not to like it. Man, all that crying. He felt something give in her face when he hit her again. It was all her fault.

He checked to make sure her man was paying attention. If he was clueless enough to be out here in no man's land in the middle of the night, he should at least have the brass to carry a gun. But the stupid asshole probably thought he could handle himself. He wanted to smack him around, but it was mighty hard to beat a man while you fucked his woman. There were only so many things a man could do properly at one time.

He relished the look on the man's face with each thrust of his dick into the woman.

# 17

NORTH FROM SAN DIEGO'S HARBOR, A LACKADAISICAL INCLINE of land culminates on the west side of Balboa Park in the community known as Hillcrest, once a scruffy mesa covered with rough chaparral. Mary Kearney obtained a deed to the land in 1870 and held it until real estate developers C. D. Arnold and D. Choate subsequently bought the property. They in turn sold it to railroad tycoon George Hill. Although Hill died in 1898 it wasn't until 1906 that William Wesley Whitson bought forty acres from the Hill estate for $115,000. Whitson, who would become known as the Father of Hillcrest, developed the area in earnest. Whitson's Hillcrest Company built forty-three homes, a sawmill, a theatre, a hotel and even a bowling alley.

Soon peppered with beautiful homes, apartment buildings, pharmacies, doctors' offices and hospitals, Hillcrest also showcased numerous "rest homes" where elderly people wiled away their final days trying not to pester their busy progeny.

As the final re-run of "I Love Lucy" pushed its way off the air in the Cloisters Home of Rest, a woman's liver-spotted hand turned off the television. She set the remote on the coffee table, stood and padded barefoot out the front door in a flannel nightgown. The sound of angry voices rang through her head as she glided toward the gate, a distance away on the grounds. The arguments always started with a woman's high-pitched assertion followed by a man's baritone response.

"She's got to go."

"I'm not abandoning her to strangers."

"She doesn't know her own name most of the time, much less who we are. And she scares the kids. Either she goes or we go. Either she goes or we go...." She heard the same phrase in her head every time she took a step.

# 18

IT WAS PAYDAY, THE DAY AT THE BEGINNING OF EVERY month that turned freshly cashed paychecks into whips that herded day workers, sailors, marines, pimps, whores and street scammers onto the downtown streets in much the same way cowpunchers whoopee ki-yo'ed those little dogies along the Wyoming trail in the old cowboy song. That was why Luke Jones and J.R. Shimmer had agreed to do a little foot patrol along lower Broadway, the six blocks west of First Avenue stretching past Front Street to Harbor Drive.

They concentrated their crime fighting efforts on the north side of the street, the one peppered with an odd commune of buildings that housed the Greyhound Bus Station, the County Court House, tattoo parlors, dilapidated hotels, strip joints and pawn shops.

"Who'd you say we're looking for again?" Luke asked.

"You must remember the guy," Shimmer said. "His real name's Brown. But you'd know him as Mr. 'Yat."

"I remember him," Luke said. "But what's he got to do with us now?"

"He's a whoremongering, drunken bum who comes down here on paydays to spend his money and get laid. Which means his wife can't buy medicine for the grandbaby and the whole bunch goes hungry for the rest of the month," Shimmer said.

"That doesn't answer my question," Luke said.

"I just sort of got in the habit of taking him home on the first of the month to help his wife out," Shimmer responded.

"Isn't that a lot like kidnapping?"

"Yeah, but he's always drunk by the time I find him, which gives me the PC I need to pick him up."

"Which doesn't give you the right to force him to go home," Luke responded. "The yellow sheets say the only options for drunks are jail, detox, or Shore Patrol for the military. You can't go around snagging people off the street and taking their liberty away."

"Don't be so self-righteous," Shimmer said. "Think of this as Devree pelting those punks with the water balloons. Sometimes you gotta break the rules to do the right thing. You'll understand once you've done the job a little longer," Shimmer said.

It was then that Luke saw an approaching sliver of a man reverse direction and scurry away, a series of guttural groans emanating from his emaciated chest.

Shimmer hustled after him. "You hold it right there, Mr. 'Yat."

"Cain't you just leave me alone for once? I'm mindin' my own bidness out here and you ain't got no right hasslin' me like this."

"You don't know what hassling is," Shimmer said. "I'm giving you the chance to do the right thing and go home to your wife and grandbaby. Course, I can clearly see you're drunk on your ass. Again. So, I guess I could take you off to jail if you'd prefer."

"I don't prefer nothin'. And another thing, my name's Brown, not 'Yat. I done tol' you that a hunnert times already."

"Your name don't matter," Shimmer responded. "What's your choice?"

"Huh?"

"Home or jail?"

"Oh, man. Home I guess, if I ain't got no other options."

"You don't know how lucky you are," Luke told him. "Almost nobody gets to choose between going home and getting tossed in jail."

"Yeah," 'Yat insisted. "But you ain't been to my home and ain't spent no time with my wife nor you wouldn't be sayin' that."

Knowing better than to challenge a subject matter expert to an argument, Luke kept his mouth shut as Shimmer guided 'Yat toward the car.

A few minutes later, Shimmer pulled the car into a crumbling driveway then knocked on a rickety screen door as he held his prisoner by the bicep. A woman with a hairdo looking like it had been arranged with a flamethrower and a flat iron pushed the door open as she dabbed at her eyes with a tissue.

"I knew you'd bring him home," she said. "So, I got a pot a' tea ready to go 'n some cookies waitin' too." She turned to her husband. "Git your sorry ass into bed while I spend a little time with some real gennelmen."

Mr. 'Yat shuffled off, shoulders stooped, his jaw tight, mumbling to himself, leaving Nadine Brown, J.R. Shimmer, and Luke Jones to settle onto an ancient set of chairs that partially surrounded an unbalanced breakfast table that rocked with every touch and made Luke wish he had a book of matches in his pocket to stick under one of its legs.

The kettle whistled a few minutes later and Luke sat silently while Mrs. Brown and J.R. Shimmer shared their monthly teatime like two long-time neighbors.

"We need to get going in just a second here," Shimmer said a few minutes into a long monologue by Mrs. Brown about what a worthless human being her once promising husband had turned out to be. "Can I take a look?"

With an air of being perpetually put-upon, the woman led the two officers down the narrow hallway to a door and tugged lightly on the handle, exposing a small room with a crib in the center and one of the dining room chairs in the corner. Moonlight, coming through a crack in the drapes, settled on a sleeping toddler who looked to be about two years old. Shimmer tiptoed in and stood over the crib. "He's getting big. Is his breathing any better?"

"He breathes pretty good when I got the proper medicine," Mrs. Brown said. As she and Shimmer backed out of the room, Shimmer pulled a twenty-dollar-bill from his pocket and slipped it into her hand.

"Now, you go on out to the car and let me get a word with your young partner here," Mrs. Brown told Shimmer when they'd reached the door." She tugged on Luke's sleeve, signaling him to stop, and waited until Shimmer was out of earshot.

"He don't like talkin' about it none, but the good Lord took his baby in a drownin' accident a while back. Did you know that?"

"I heard something about it," Luke said.

"He a good man's what I'm tryin' to say. That's all, just wanted you to know. Cuzz I think he be misunderstood sometimes."

Luke looked at his Seiko runner's watch as he stepped into the night. It was 12:00, the stroke of midnight. A fitting time for an epiphany about the essence of the man whose life he'd frequently regretted saving.

Tree roots pushed dirt through the grass near the side of the house where a corroded aluminum trashcan overflowed onto the grass parkway. Shimmer stooped several times, picked up the trash, tossed it in and secured the lid. Stepping back, he felt a sickening squish beneath his boot and raising his foot released the nasty stink of dog shit. "Ah, man," he said. "That's bullshit."

"Bullshit, out here?" Luke asked with a grin.

"Bullshit's only an expression," Shimmer shot back. "A big steaming pile of dog shit's what is what it actually is. It's totally fucked up is what it is. Like I said, it's total bullshit."

"I think you were right the first time," Luke said. "It's most likely bullshit."

"It's totally fucked up is what it is," Shimmer repeated.

Luke let a short beat pass. "You know," he said, "now I think of it, it's probably not shit after all. It looks more to me like you're melting."

Shimmer shot Luke a go fuck yourself expression before the two men started to laugh in unison.

# 19

AFTER DROPPING LUKE AT HIS PATROL UNIT, SHIMMER guided the steering wheel one-handed, backing his car into Balboa Park's "Slot," a patch of pavement left over from construction of the freeway intersection of Interstate 5 and State Highway 163. Jutting about 40 yards in the direction of nowhere, the Slot sat hidden by high brush to the north and corralled by a chain-link fence to the west. The protection provided by the freeways, natural vegetation, and fencing made it a perfect spot for hiding out to write reports far from the nosy intrusions of John Q. Citizen.

Within minutes, although Shimmer could never sleep well at home, sleep started tugging on his eyelids like muscular arms pulling a sail into place. As he battled to stay awake, haunting memories crawled inside the fog of his half-awake brain.

He wasn't alone. An old woman lay on the other side of the fence as his breathing slowed and he lost his battle to stay awake. Although the old lady saw his body, she couldn't see his unconscious spirit leaning through the car door to observe his laboring body. She had no way of knowing about the recurring dream that haunted his brief moments of tortuous sleep.

*The heavy breathing on the other end of the line didn't command the po-*
*lice operator's attention. Lord knows, they heard enough of that. What really*
*brought her alert was the gurgling in the background and the chilling whim-*
*pers heard away from the phone as a woman choked and sobbed and counted.*
*"One, two, three..."*

*"Sir, can I have your name and address?" The question would likely force*
*a hang up if the call was a crank.*

*"The name's William Turnbow and the address is in what I've heard one*
*of your people crassly refer to as 'the nut-job file.' The bitch whining in the*
*background is my wife Sarah. And she's got to the count of 300 to live."*

*"I'm sending units, sir," the operator said as she pushed the console button,*
*alerting the sergeant in the radio room to pick up and initiate a three-way*
*connection. She typed, directing the caller's information to the radio dis-*
*patcher as her supervisor cued in.*

*The dispatcher broadcast the call while the sergeant monitored her phone*
*and the radio frequency, ready to alert responding units to any late-breaking*
*details.*

*"Why are you doing this to your wife, sir?" the operator asked.*

*"Twelve, thirteen, fourteen..." The dispatcher could barely discern the*
*counted numbers through the tortured crying and choking that crackled*
*through her headset.*

*"Can I speak with your wife, sir?"*

*"Twenty, twenty-one, twenty-two..."*

*"Do you mind telling me what room you're in?"*

*"Twenty-six, twenty-seven, twenty-eight..." The phone clicked dead.*

*The operator tried getting Turnbow back on the line, every ring replacing*
*a counted number as no one picked up.*

*The sergeant in the radio room heard Officer Shimmer announce his ar-*
*rival at the scene and ask if there were any additional details.*

*"Negative, five-John. She should be well over a hundred by now, but the*
*reporting party's hung up."*

*"Ten-4, do you have an ETA on my cover units?"*

*"Thirteen-John's stuck in accident traffic and my other units are all out of service on priority calls," the dispatcher said.*

*Shimmer turned his portable radio down and jogged to the front of the house where he ducked under the paint splattered windows. He pressed his ear against the flimsy door and heard a woman coughing, choking and pleading for her life as she counted. The smell of burnt bacon drifted under the door as Shimmer heard a thud followed by the sound of something like a sack of potatoes dropping against the floor.*

*"You better stay down this time. You screwed up my breakfast for the last time you stupid cow," the man on the other side of the door said. "And, you keep missing the count." He prompted her, "two-hundred-eighty-three, two-hundred-eighty-four. You better keep up or I'll cut you right now."*

*Sarah started her count again. "Two-hundred-and-eighty-five, two-hundred-and-eighty-six-- You don't have to do this."*

*Shimmer only had a few moments to make his move or the woman would almost certainly die while he stood on the other side of the door and did nothing.*

*"Two-hundred-and-ninety-eight, two-hundred..."*

*He missed the latch as he kicked. His boot caught in the flimsy door, leaving him bouncing on a single leg. If the caller had wanted to, he could have killed Shimmer in that instant as he dangled in the doorway like a helpless marionette. But the man intended to kill his wife and die in the attempt.*

*Shimmer jerked free and cork-screwed for a clear shot, twirling in the air as he pulled the trigger. A bullet pierced the man's chest as the knife slashed into the woman's neck. Shimmer tumbled in a heap onto the plank floor.*

*The trio's fate had been sealed the instant Turnbow's bacon started to burn.*

# 20

IT HAD BEEN HOURS SINCE THE RESIDENT OF THE Cloister's Home of
Rest turned off the TV, forgot her name again, stood from her vinyl re-
cliner, and walked into the jumbled memories of her past. Her evening
walk had started like all the others, an innocent ramble through the
scented rows of roses in the backyard garden. But as she passed beneath
the arbor and onto the sidewalk, she entered the place where memories
of past loves and former ambitions jumbled into a mental tangle of
confusion.

In the mélange of fractured memories, time and place formed a
jagged mental jigsaw, and she wandered along a descending path getting more and more lost in the heart of Balboa Park.

Tears rimmed her eyes and the flames of pain that riffled through
her chest wheezed out of her nostrils. After about an hour, she fell exhausted to the ground and started creeping along on her knees until
she fell to the ground and decided to die rather than struggle to move
another inch. She'd lost all sense of time but eventually saw a police car
a little ways off in the distance. The sight of that car was enough in-
centive to push herself to her knees again and crawl toward the salva-
tion it represented. She had a pretty good head of steam on until she
was confronted by a previously unseen chain link fence. The sight of it
made her lose heart and fall to the dirt again.

She almost certainly would have died there except she spied a tear at the base of the fence which gave her the strength she needed to gather herself and crawl through it toward the officer in the car who could save her life.

# 21

THE HOOD OF SHIMMER'S CAR BOUNCED AND THE JOLT of it pushed through his mental fog, reminding him that he was sleeping on duty in Balboa Park. In the last instant of his dream, he had yanked his gun and squeezed its trigger killing Turnbow once again and watching Turnbow's wife die at his feet. In the real world, he'd punched outward and smashed the fragile flesh of his hand against the windshield, breaking a bone in his hand.

The pain brought instant clarity and helped him to understand his predicament as he saw a woman's brittle body splayed across the hood of his car. He snorted the guttural sounds of an animal in pain through tobacco stained teeth as he reached with his healthy hand to open the door. Holding his throbbing hand close against his torso, he stumbled out of the car, and checked the old woman's pulse. Each shallow breath seemed a noiseless struggle against death, barely moving the flimsy nightshirt covering her body.

Shimmer considered his limited options. Calling for help was out of the question. Telling the truth would get him suspended without pay for sleeping on duty. His only hope for aiding the woman, and staying out of trouble at the same time, lay in moving her near the fence and fabricating a reason for finding her there.

Every movement added to the throbbing and swelling of his hand as he lifted her from the hood and carried her to the fence. Once there he knelt and set her on a heap of leaves then pulled his handi-talkie from its leather holder on his gun belt. "Unit Fifty-two John," he said. "I need a supervisor and an additional unit at the Slot in Balboa Park."

# 22

Sergeant Biletnikoff set his cup down in the watch commander's office, interrupting a big fish tale he'd been telling the slack-jawed Deputy Chief Browner who owned the bass voice of a movie hero but whose well-earned reputation included a penchant for unfair treatment of the troops. Like any baseball umpire notorious for making bad calls, Browner was a known quantity. Most seasoned officers were afraid of his overweening ambition and foul temperament and anticipated that he'd screw them over if a citizen filed a complaint.

Biletnikoff actually liked Browner, but only because he was too ambitious and too stupid to recognize how the senior executive used and manipulated him. "I wonder what Shimmer's stepped into this time," Biletnikoff said. "He may be the biggest pain in the ass who's ever worked for me."

"He's a whiner sure enough," Browner agreed before feigning a high-pitched mocking voice. "Why're you giving me that beat again? I can't make my numbers up there. You're always putting me on graveyard and you know how I hate graveyard. Why can't you just leave me alone and let me do my job? He's worse than my thirteen-year-old kid."

"He's part of Lt. Rood's crowd these days, which would be bad, except he's easy to manipulate and we can use him to our advantage," Biletnikoff said.

"You don't think he'd actually help you undermine that self-righteous bitch?" Browner said.

"He didn't know it at the time, but he was instrumental in helping me get rid of Durango," Biletnikoff responded. "I know he's been tough to control ever since Jones saved his life, but I know how he ticks. I'll turn him in our direction again when we need him."

"That hot stop Jones initiated the other day made us look pretty good in the media," Browner replied. "He may be obnoxious, but he's a sharp kid."

Biletnikoff grunted; a non-verbal, ostensibly safe, means of discounting Browner's comment. "Jones got lucky. It's that simple. But people are acting like he's Jesus sailing back on the clouds. Putting a wedge between Shimmer and Jones will be the answer we need when the time comes."

# 23

BOB FIEDLER PICKED UP THE MICROPHONE WHEN Biletnikoff came up on the tactical frequency. "Go ahead, Sarge," he said.

"We're meeting Shimmer at the Slot. Where is that exactly?" Biletnikoff asked.

Fiedler knew that virtually every officer on frequency-4 had switched to TAC to audit the conversation and divulging the Slot's secret location to Biletnikoff while other officers listened was a decidedly unpleasant prospect. The Slot was one of those select places where officers could safely avoid the public when working graveyard, and exposing the clandestine location to Biletnikoff was the last thing Fiedler wanted to do.

"Well, Sarge, explaining it's a little complicated. Since I'm almost there, why don't I save you the trip and evaluate this thing for you?"

"I'm already en route," Biletnikoff said. "Just stay on TAC and guide me in."

Fiedler could almost hear the collective groans of the tuned-in officers as he gave out the directions. His being manipulated into publicly revealing the location of the Slot to the least trusted sergeant in the division made for a truly shitty moment. The situation couldn't possibly have a happy ending and, to make matters worse, Biletnikoff would be pulling into the Slot behind him in just a few minutes.

Fiedler found Shimmer on his knees, cradling an ancient wisp of a woman as Biletnikoff pulled his cruiser in next to Fiedler's car in time to take in Shimmer's award winning performance.

As Biletnikoff approached on foot, Shimmer gave an exaggerated grimace and blurted, "Hey Sarge, I think I broke my hand or something."

"What happened?" Biletnikoff asked as Fiedler walked up behind him and peered over his shoulder at Shimmer, exposing a raised eyebrow apparently designed to express his disapproval of the whole situation.

"Nothin' was happenin' up on the hill," Shimmer began.

"Wait a second," Biletnikoff interrupted. "I bet this is the rest home walkaway we had the all units about."

"Yeah, that's what I figure, too," Shimmer said pretending knowledge of information broadcast while he slept. "I decided to check the park since I already looked all over my beat for her. I pulled real slow in here with my windows down just like you taught me, and heard sort of a cry, I guess. I shined my searchlight around, thought I seen somethin' and checked it out. Poor old lady, all I could think of was to pick her up and get her home, but I slipped and couldn't break the fall with her in my arms."

Biletnikoff and Shimmer turned to find the source of an exaggerated sniffling sound and saw Fiedler tucking his Tuffy jacket's arms around the woman's torso.

"Is there a problem, Fiedler," Biletnikoff asked.

"I don't think so," Fiedler assured him. "Although, do either of you smell rotten fish?"

Both Shimmer and Biletnikoff ignored him.

"I was bein' careful," Shimmer said, "but I tripped over this log while I was carrying her to the car. I got my flashlight in my hand, and as I'm fallin', all I can think of is 'don't hurt the old lady'."

Shimmer glanced toward his feet and found a nearby stone. "I guess I hit my hand on this when I hit the ground." He toe-kicked the stone and the sound of the rock rolling on pavement punctuated the image.

"It hurts like a sonofabitch, Sarge."

"Didn't I tell you, not to use that kind of language on the job any-more?" Biletnikoff demanded.

"I know Sarge, it just hurts so damn bad," Shimmer went on. "I was in so much pain I could barely move till I finally managed to stand up when you got here. I gotta say, I'm surprised as hell that she's still alive."

"Yeah, I'd say she's goddamned lucky you were on the case," Fiedler agreed as he flashed a facetious smile that he followed with another pronounced sniff. He poked Shimmer on the upper leg with the antenna of his flashlight, wanting his attention so he could tell him what an impressive award-caliber performance he was giving, but Shimmer refused to acknowledge him.

In the meantime, no one made a move to get the old lady any real help.

"If you two'll quit your preaching about saying bad words and brag-gin' on your outstanding policing techniques and kissin' up like a punk kid at his school teacher's desk, maybe we should think about getting the old lady some help."

Fiedler waited several seconds for the sergeant to process the situation and tell Shimmer he was full of shit.

"Well, it's damn good police work is what it is," Biletnikoff said finally. "See what I told you about driving slow and keeping all your windows open. You never know what you might find."

"Yeah, Sarge, that was good advice all right," Shimmer acknowledged.

Fiedler couldn't believe what he was hearing, Had the Sarge lost his mind? A Shimmer-Biletnikoff love-in? No way. He was tempted to look around for a reconstituted Candid Camera crew, thinking the whole thing had to be a set up with him as the patsy.

Fiedler finally stepped in when Biletnikoff failed to come up with a plan to help the old lady. "Hey, why don't you drive Shimmer over to Centre City for X-rays and get started on the injury reports? Call an ambulance to take gramma here over to Community's ER so the doc can make sure Shimmer's droppin' her didn't kill her. The ambulance crew and I'll figure out a way to get Shimmer's car back to the garage. Then we can contact, what's the name of that rest home she walked away from?"

Fiedler stared at Shimmer, waiting for an answer he knew Shimmer didn't know, and thought the Sarge might finally figure the whole odd fiction out.

Biletnikoff staved off the impasse. "It was the Cloisters, wasn't it?"

"Yeah, that's it," Shimmer agreed. "I'm pretty sure it was the Cloisters."

Fiedler shook his head, trying to clear the air around him. Thirty minutes before he'd have laid odds the worst thing he'd encounter during the shift was missing dinner. But now the Sarge had obviously lost his mind.

Fiedler turned his attention to the moaning woman as Biletnikoff headed for his car with Shimmer limping along beside him looking like the pain had suddenly transferred to his leg. The effect was marvelously dramatic.

"Let's get you to the ER," Biletnikoff told Shimmer. "Fiedler here can look after your vehicle until someone comes for it since he has to wait for the ambulance anyway."

Shimmer limped to Beltinikoff's car and lowered himself in delicately, looking like his whole body was in a sling.

Fiedler, who'd strolled over behind them, wondered if maybe the injury had miraculously relocated to Shimmer's torso. The night only got more bizarre when Biletnikoff told Shimmer he could expect an official commendation for superior work as the sergeant shut Shimmer's door.

"Yeah, you bet its nice work," Fiedler said as he dug the heel of his boot into the soft ground. What a night. The Slot got blown. Biletnikoff had officially lost his mind and Shimmer put himself in line for a commendation by being too worthless for words. Fiedler sniffed exaggeratedly again and spoke into the night. "I still don't know though, you two sure you don't smell a dead fish around here somewhere?"

# 24

BELITNIKOFF DROPPED BY DEPUTY CHIEF BROWNER'S OFFICE the next afternoon before holding lineup. "Sorry to disturb you again, Sir," he said as soon as the secretary had passed him through. "But I think you're going to like this one. I'm pretty sure Shimmer was asleep in a remote part of Balboa Park last night. Somehow he managed to rescue an elderly lady who'd walked away from a rest home, and to break his hand in the process."

"I'm sure the story he's telling about how it all happened is phony somehow, but dispatch had been broadcasting an all units for the rest home walkaway, so we can get some good media coverage about how our cops are always looking out for the little guy. It'll help counter balance the beating we've been taking about the rape series we have going on up at Northern Division."

"That's sounds real good," Browner said. "I'll coordinate with press relations about finding the old lady."

Biletnikoff nodded.

"It also sounds like some sort of commendation might be in order, don't you think?" Browner continued.

"I'm going to write that up tonight and have it ready for Lt. Rood's signature tomorrow," Biletnikoff said.

Browner shook his head. "It's a bullshit commendation and she'll see right through it. Why don't you bring it on over for me to sign.

Then you and I can make a big production out of presenting it to him in lineup for a little payback about the way Coleman and Rood handled that promotion situation." Browner settled back in his chair with a self-satisfied grin. Then he decided to pass on a verbal attaboy to his current favorite toady. "Good work, Lieutenant," he said even though, given the state of his relationship with the Chief, he probably had zero power to push Biletnikoff out of a plane, let alone engineer a promotion.

"Thank you, Chief," Belitnikoff said.

# 25

As Luke walked behind Denny and Hank Hunter, undulating lights spanked the walls of the thrumming interior of Crystal T's Emporium, one of the most popular discos. It was a total mystery to him how the incessant thumping of bass speakers that blasted insipid music in sync with intermittent orgasms of light splashing against the walls could work so effectively as a human aphrodisiac.

Legitimate conversation was impossible. The watered down drinks were a waste of time and money and, worse yet, not once had Luke encountered a woman in one of these joints who'd sparked any interest in his seeing her again. Short dresses and low-cut tops seemed nothing more than camouflage for their spectacular public bubble-headedness.

Luke didn't have a clue how to dance. He certainly couldn't gyrate to Donna Summer or the Bee Gees, and the song detonating the air now, the one by The Village People that constantly repeated the letters "YMCA," what the heck was that all about?

Luke loved the music of Michael Franks, James Taylor, Jackson Brown and Joanie Mitchell. Singer/songwriters were his cup of tea. Maybe he could fake a little movement in the middle of the crowded dance floor if one of their songs unexpectedly made the disco's play list but that never happened.

What the hell. He'd promised Denny he'd come along. But this was absolutely the last time.

Denny loved giving his dance floor performances as much as he loved the ones he orchestrated in bed. Evidence indicated he was equally good at both. He could certainly out Travolta John Travolta in the vertical glide, and constantly coaxed women off of the dance floor and into his bed where the two of them would do the horizontal hump once the disco lights had dimmed.

Hank Hunter, Luke's fellow sufferer, didn't seem interested in dancing with anyone other than his wife, and she'd taken advantage of her stewardess's benefits to whisk their baby girl off to visit her parents in Florida. At least Luke would have company at the table this time, even if he was stuck in an environment with zero opportunity to hold anything approaching a real conversation with anybody.

Not that Hank had said much since he'd arrived at their apartment to pick them up. Since Hunter always appeared at ease, Luke couldn't tell if he actually wanted to go to the disco or was tagging along just to please Denny the same way Luke did. He'd shaken their hands, used Denny's bathroom, decided the evening was too warm for his jacket and excused himself to put it in the trunk of his car before the trio took off for Denny's planned festivities.

On the positive side, Denny'd probably find a horizontal mambo partner in short order, which would free Luke and Hunter to get the hell out of there and grab a bite to eat.

And then Luke saw Her and his pulse rate soared. He'd seen her before, but not in a disco. He'd watched her play Perdita in *A Winter's Tale* at the Old Globe Theatre. But this time, her low-slung, electric blue mini-skirt sliding against long, tanned legs instantly transformed her from mere woman into a Goddess.

She danced to the Village People's ridiculous lyrics, but her graceful movements set her apart from the hodgepodge of twitchy, jerking bodies surrounding her on the dance floor. Her russet hair looked like

Russian sable, emanating a magnetic animal glow around her face, setting off luminous eyes.

He knew he should look away as she turned in his direction, but he didn't. He'd never been this forward before, but she was a stunner and an excellent actress to boot. What, he wondered, had brought her to such an insipid place?

She'd stopped dancing and was moving toward him, her gaze commanding his eyes, her determined expression commanding him not to go anywhere. As she approached the table, Luke shifted his weight, ready to stand for a greeting.

He was sure how it would go. She wouldn't say anything. She'd simply take his hand and lead him to the center of the dance floor. This time, his feet wouldn't forget how to move. His body would glide next to hers in an erotic embrace. He'd hold her close and she'd quote something from Shakespeare into his ear.

Then she was at the table, reaching her hand out for--Hunter. "I noticed you haven't found a dance partner, how about me?" she said.

Watching Hunter confidently rise and take her hand was a surreal thing. Air leaked from Luke's body like a balloon bleeding slowly at the valve. Losing out to him at the Academy was one thing, but this was too much. Then he heard Hunter's smooth voice booming over the noise.

"My wife couldn't join us tonight and I only dance with her, but I'm sure my friend Luke here would love to take my place."

Luke's inclination not to accept the role of second fiddle evaporated as quickly as the light of her smile splashed on his face.

He stood and extended his hand. "I'm Luke Jones," he said.

"I'm Sib--"

"Sibyl Vane," Luke said. "I know.

"How could you possibly know that?"

"I've seen you at the Globe," Luke told her. "Is your name something you selected for the stage or the one your parents gave you?"

"I was born with it," Sibyl answered.

"I take it your mother's an actress and a fan of Oscar Wilde," Luke said.

"Yes, but--"

Luke interrupted with a monologue about Sibyl Vane from Oscar Wilde's *The Picture of Dorian Gray.*

> I have been right, Basil, haven't I, to take my love out
> of poetry and find my wife in Shakespeare's plays. Lips
> that Shakespeare taught to speak have whispered their
> secret in my ear. I have had the arms of Rosalind
> around me and kissed Juliet on the mouth.

Sibyl took Luke's hand to lead him to the dance floor, prompting him to switch from quoting Wilde to uttering the words of Lord Byron:

> She walks in beauty, like the night
> Of cloudless climes and starry skies,
> And all that best of dark and bright
> Meets in her aspect and her eyes...

"Where have you been all my life?" Sibyl asked as she put her arm around his waist and guided him to the middle of the crowded dance floor.

# 26

"HELLO, LUKE. HOW ARE YOU?"

The sounds entering Luke's head were a little fuzzy, but he was sure he could see Dr. Pantages standing at the foot of his bed. "I'm fine Doctor and yourself?"

"I'm always fine."

"What brings you here at this ungodly hour?" Luke asked.

"I've got a meeting with Chief Coleman in the other room, but he's running late so I told Donna I'd come over here and wait," Pantages replied.

"I see," Luke said. Although relieved, he was left with his unanswered question about why the psychiatrist didn't wait in the Chief's outer office.

"I sometimes wander around in the middle of the night and check up on the rank and file as they sleep," Dr. Pantages said. "I've been doing it ever since the PSA crash."

"Admirable, doctor," Luke said, blinking. "But it makes me feel a little like a lab rat."

Pantages' return smile was somber. "I'm not surprised that's how you interpret it. But it's actually not that way at all. I'm charged with the mental health of everyone on the department. You know these people as well as I do. Don't you think it's important to check up on them when they least expect it?"

Luke nodded.

"Have you been journaling like I asked you to?" Pantages asked.

This was starting to get tedious again, just like that time in her office.

Luke rolled onto his side, intent on settling into a deeper sleep. But he woke up instead. He kicked the covers off and headed toward the kitchen to pour a tumbler of the ten-year-old Laphroaig scotch Hartson had introduced him too. At least his binging was getting a bit more elegant.

# 27

LUKE TOOK HIS ISLAY STYLE SINGLE MALT SCOTCH together with a pen and paper onto the balcony. He had no idea if the Dr. Pantages of his dreams was right about his having to get in touch with his feelings, but he had discovered that he actually enjoyed keeping a journal.

The silence that surrounded him fit his laconic personality perfectly. San Diego's famous June gloom, a month of low-hanging clouds and cool temperatures, had dissipated right on time, the first day of July, and the light glow of the late afternoon had brought bathers to the pool beneath him. Several buxom women relaxed in the loungers that fringed the pool, their accented pulchritude making Luke reflect on the function of love and how poorly it had served him in his life. He took the cap off his pen and started to write.

*I met Isabelle when we were high school sophomores and fell for her as I imagine only a fifteen year old boy can fall – fast and hard. I'm pretty sure she cared for me, but I never seemed to measure up to her family's standards and she was always looking for someone better. Every time I gave up on her and started dating someone else, she'd insist on reverting to an exclusive relationship. I always agreed, reluctantly, and the new arrangement would last just long enough for her to get bored again. The resulting ennui always resulted in her following her sisters' advice to seek out a more deserving boyfriend.*

*I was a total sap, and the worst part is, I can't think why I kept taking her back. In part, I suppose, it was because she always made me feel like she was taking me back. The funny part is, now I can't imagine what I saw in her that made me fall so hard. The only explanation may be that we were fifteen years old.*

*She and her eight older sisters formed a stunning group of beautiful and accomplished young women. Two were physicians, one was a junior in college and another was finishing up her doctorate in astrophysics. The one who was a high school senior was poised to follow the well-established family tradition of becoming the class valedictorian.*

*Hard as it is to believe now, Isabelle was the orchid among the daisies. Even at fifteen, she had the best body of the nine and the whole bunch was gorgeous. I used to think she had a great disposition too, at least until I got to know her better. That's when I finally figured out that nothing great can be built on a foundation of lies. I guess the simple explanation is that I wanted to believe her because I couldn't comprehend her interest in me.*

# 28

On his day off, Luke passed through the Northern Division squad room on his way to meet Sergeant T.D. Hartson and spotted Hank Hunter sitting at the line-up table. Hunter lifted his chin toward the sergeant's office to indicate the location of Luke's mentor.

The new sergeant had a phone pressed to his ear, a hand in a file drawer and his back to the door. Luke interpreted the signals to mean that Hartson was too busy to be interrupted and retreated back to the squad room to take a seat next to Hunter.

"How'd you enjoy that meat market the other night?" he asked as he pulled a chair from beneath the table.

"OK, I guess, even though it's no more my scene than yours," Hunter answered. "The Sarge had something come up, so it looks like your ride with him tonight's gone up in smoke. He said you could ride with me if you want."

"I'd like to say hello before we go," Luke responded. "Do we need to get going right away?"

"It'll take me a few minutes to load up the car," Hunter said as Luke walked back toward the sergeant's office.

Hartson noticed Luke at the doorway as he hung up the phone. "I expect Hunter's told you something's come up. I can pick you up a little later if you don't mind riding with him for a while."

"Riding with him is fine. But he didn't say what came up?" The inflection in Luke's voice rose to make sure that Hartson understood it was a question.

"I know you've heard about this guy raping women at the beach. I passed along a tip to the sex crimes supervisor who's wanting a meet for some additional information. In fact, it would help me out if I could pick your brain about a few things for a report I'll be submitting in the next few days."

"I don't know anything about the rape series." Luke said. "How can I help?"

Hartson assured Luke that he'd fill him in later and hurried off to his car with briefcase in hand.

Luke joined his academy classmate in his squad car and the two of them patrolled Hunter's beat for a while. The only sounds in the cab chirruped out from the police radio until Hunter finally asked about Sybil.

"You seemed a bit love-clobbered by that woman at the disco the other night," Hunter said. His assertion was accompanied by a mischievous smirk.

"She is something, don't you think?" Luke said.

"She is really something. I'll tell you what, if I wasn't married, I'd have..." Hunter paused to allow his smile to say more than any words could convey.

"You'd have what?" Luke asked.

Hunter laughed. "It's a good thing I'm married. I don't have a clue what to do with an unattached beauty like her these days."

"The way she singled you out in that crowd? I don't expect the two of you would've wasted much time figuring things out. Do you know who she is?" Luke asked.

"Should I?"

"Her name's Sibyl Vane. She's an actress. I've seen her at the Old Globe."

"We don't get to many plays," Hunter said. "Has she been on TV?"

"A couple shows so far." Luke pondered the life of a married couple with a young child and the reality of not getting out much. "I hope I'll still have time to go to the theater when I'm married with kids," he said.

"Priorities do change a lot," Hunter said. "They basically trim down to a select few things you want to share with your wife and kid, and the rest of your time is spent at work."

The dispatcher interrupted Luke's response with an assignment to "meet the RP at the corner of Governor Drive and Genesee Street." The reporting party would direct Hunter to the location of the domestic disturbance call from there.

As Hunter neared the wide intersection, a woman emerged from the darkness into the light emanating from a streetlamp on the southeast corner. At least sixty years old, she wore navy slacks, a turquoise shirt, and a black, zip-up sweater. Her gray, jaw-length hair was noticeably flattened on one side of her head.

Hunter pulled the car next to her and, as he and Luke got out, the reason for her lopsided look became immediately apparent as she repeatedly ran splayed fingers through the flat side of her hair. "Officers—it's quiet now—but I just... Well, it sounded like he was killing her—and he gets real mad if one of us neighbors calls you – but I just had to. I asked you to meet me here so maybe he won't figure out which one of us called you," she added, obviously believing the few extra words explained more than they actually did.

"Ma'am, let's start with your name to verify that I'm responding to the call I was dispatched to."

"I'm Joanie. My husband's Winslow."

"Joanie and Winslow, English. Is that correct?"

Once the woman verified that Hunter was correct, he drew a nexus between her name and several calls she'd made to dispatch over the past months to report domestic violence at her next door neighbor's house.

"Winslow won't call anymore and he doesn't like me to call either. He says it's none of our business. But I think he won't call because he's afraid of Rivers."

"Afraid of Rivers?" Hunter asked.

"Oh dear, I'm not making this easy, am I?" She stopped running her fingers through her hair and started nervously stretching the bottom of her sweater.

"It's all right, ma'am," Hunter said, his soothing manner allowing her to relax enough to speak clearly.

"George Rivers. He beats his wife and screams and cusses something awful when she calls out for help. It's just awful, and to think…"

"We'd better not delay any longer," Hunter insisted. "We'll need the Rivers' exact address though." After Mrs. English provided the information, Hunter told her they'd check the situation out and asked her to go home ahead of their arrival at the Rivers' house.

"Thank you, Officer," Mrs. English answered before disappearing into the darkness of the closed gas station and opening the door to her white BMW.

Hunter soon pulled the patrol car up in front of a large white house with a red-tiled roof, a perfectly trimmed yard, and impeccably manicured shrubbery. There were no dead fronds on any of the palm trees and the house decor visible through the windows was spotless. The window frames were a freshly painted dark red that Luke decided were almost certainly a perfect match for the spanking new roof tiles as Hunter rang the doorbell.

The officers waited a minute or so before Hunter rang the doorbell again. He followed up by pounding on the door with a demand to be allowed inside.

A pale woman with hair the color of mottled strawberries and a palpably timid demeanor finally opened the door. Her fair skin could easily have formed freckles, but the lack of discoloration on her face indicated that she stayed inside most of the time or wore heavy sunscreen when she ventured outside. Her coloring and even features would have combined to make her enigmatically gorgeous except for a large bruise along her cheek and beneath her left ear.

Clearly physically fit, she wore a white shirtwaist dress with small yellow polka dots and a white belt. A matching bow pulled a little of her hair away from her stunning face. She looked to be in her late twenties, but the question of age was muddied by the swelling and darkening bruise on the face and her blue eyes that were puffy and reddened from an obvious bout of prolonged crying.

Her voice was hoarse. "What're the police doing here?"

"Are you all right, ma'am?" Hunter asked. "We got a call about screaming and what sounded like violence coming from this address."

"Screaming? From here?" she shook her head insistently. "No way."

"What happened to your face, ma'am?" Hunter asked.

"Is this something you have to do now? My husband hasn't been home from work long and I don't want to disturb him. He works hard and needs time to unwind."

"We don't want to disturb you, ma'am, but we do have to check the complaint out since I can see a fresh injury. Besides that, I know my beat partners have come to your house several times recently on domestic violence calls," Hunter insisted.

"This?" She touched her face and smiled weakly. "I fell down the steps." She turned toward the interior of the house, opening the door for the officers to see the tidy interior and pointed to the stairway. The clean carpet was free of even a speck of debris, which, to the uninitiated, would leave the impression that the behavior of the occupants was as tidy as their home.

"Honey, can you come here," she turned her head and raised her voice. Palm prints were visible on her throat. The sound of someone approaching from the adjacent room could clearly be heard.

Mrs. Rivers asked a question of the approaching husband before he reached the hallway. "These officers are saying someone heard screaming tonight coming from our house. Did I scream when I fell?"

A man who looked like a male counterpart to the attractive wife appeared in the doorway. At least as physically fit as the woman, his bronze complexion and beach blonde hair left the impression that he spent a good deal of his free time at the water, most probably riding a surfboard.

"I'm always telling you to be more careful," Mr. Rivers said as he slithered an arm around his wife's waist and drew her hand into his. Luke noted the initial resistance, but she relented a few seconds after her husband started openly displaying affection.

"I'd be willing to bet that old battle-axe, Mrs. English, called you?" his raised inflection indicated that what he'd said was a question.

Neither of the officers responded.

"She just can't stop minding our business," Rivers continued, "She hates me for some reason and calls in false reports when she gets bored." He stopped talking to assess the officers' reaction but got none from either of them.

"Isn't it a crime to make a false report, Officer? Why don't you run her in and leave us alone?"

A toddler wearing blue pajamas with rocket ships racing toward distant planets soon appeared to wrap himself around the woman's legs. A second boy, probably a year older, silently came to her side an instant later. His red pajamas were sports themed and covered with players and paraphernalia of various games.

Both boys, miniscule versions of their mother, were soon wispy vines encircling her legs. Their hair and skin were mini versions of hers, and their icy blue eyes could have been reflections from her mirror.

Hunter's tone turned curt and dismissive as soon as the boys came to the door. "Fine, I just need everyone's names for my daily journal so I can leave." Every ounce of compassion had instantly disappeared, transforming him into a human replica of desiccated driftwood. Without personally witnessing it, Luke would never have believed Hunter was capable of such distant behavior toward an obvious victim.

"I'm Pam Rivers and this is my husband, George."

"That's roger, ida, virginia, edward, roger, sam?" Hunter verified the spelling of the last name using the SDPD phonetic alphabet.

"Yes, that's right."

"And the boys?" Hunter asked.

Mrs. Rivers cupped the oldest boy's chin. "This is Bradley and the younger one's Alan."

"We're done here," Hunter told Luke, his disgust unrestrained. Then he led the way to the patrol car. "Man, I hate domestic disturbance calls, especially when the victims lie to our faces and kids are involved. There's no way she got that bruise accidentally falling down the steps, and I bet he hurts her in front of those kids."

Luke didn't know a single cop who liked handling family disturbance calls since there was virtually no way for somebody to emerge from the situation with a win. There was never a decent witness and the victim almost never acknowledged the abuse. All an officer could do was show up, talk to those involved, expect a series of lies, then leave prepared to write and submit a report full of lies and half-truths with a cover note explaining their suspicions to the detectives. Most cops had chosen their careers to help others, but domestic violence calls almost always precluded them from being able to help anyone. Still, Luke felt Hunter's anger was over the top given the circumstances, since Mrs. Rivers' stonewalling was to be expected.

Luke wondered why so many women stuck up for their husbands or boyfriends under recurring abuse. The only things that made sense were for the woman to take advantage of the help offered by the police, leave with the kids, and prosecute the abusive male partner. The dynamics clearly involved something other than love, and Luke would have taken odds that Mrs. Rivers had no way to support two little boys without her husband and couldn't access any real family support. What sense did it make for an officer to get angry and leave her with a sense of hopelessness, instead of somehow signaling an interest in trying to help?

# 29

"IT WAS A GOOD SUGGESTION COMING HERE," LUKE said as he swallowed another bite of pepperoni pizza. One of a local chain of restaurants started in the fifties, the original Filippi's was a little north of downtown but this Garnet Avenue installation made it easier for people living in Pacific Beach to enjoy the popular Italian food. It kept the original's basic décor. The flickering illumination in the dark interior emanated from candles that rested on red and white checked tablecloths.

"This is one of my favorite places," Hunter told him before he took another slice off the round, metal serving tray.

"Sorry I got so pissed back there," Hunter said. "I shouldn't let it get to me."

Luke took a sip of his soda. "Women and kids getting abused is the worst," he said.

Hunter nodded in assent before he spoke. "I can't understand a victim creating all that misery when there's plenty to go around already."

"Why are you blaming the wife?" Luke asked. "What did she do other than try to protect herself and her kids?"

"I can't explain it really," Hunter said. "But, life is constantly crashing down on unsuspecting people. I can't figure out why some create more drama in their lives by letting abusive people into their homes and then refusing to do anything about it."

Luke leaned forward and put his elbows on the table as Hunter glanced furtively towards the front door. "Your indignation's aimed at the wrong place," Luke said before settling back into his chair. Hunter's nervous reaction made him feel that leaning forward was too aggressive a move for the situation.

Hunter scratched his left forearm before balling his hands into fists, pushing them against the vinyl of the booth and shifting his weight. "She should take the kids and leave him," he said with a growing hint of nervousness or anger in his voice. Luke wasn't sure which.

"She's most likely got nowhere to go and no one she can trust to help her," Luke said. His words were intended as a palliative suggestion, but he realized they sounded more like a pronouncement of judgment which probably accounted for Hunter's discomfort. "Let's talk about something else. How about telling me something about your baseball career?"

Hunter groaned. "I hate talking about it because it's so painful," he said. "I'd rather be playing baseball than doing anything else. But since I've got no choice, I keep looking for other ways to enjoy the game. I tell my wife I need a son so I can coach his team and live vicariously through him."

Luke grinned. "It sounds like you've worked out the perfect solution."

"My wife always asks what I'd do if we had a son who didn't like baseball. I tell her it'd be grounds for divorce since it would be proof the kid wasn't mine."

"How long have you two been married?" Luke asked.

"Eight laugh-a-minute, years of pure joy," he said. "I'm a lucky guy. She's stood by me through my baseball travel, my injury, the academy and all these weird patrol hours. None of it's been easy.

"The majors can be great money once you're established, but couples spend a lot of time apart and I didn't last long enough in the show to make the big bucks. I think it's not as lonely for her now that we have Sheila. But my injury--" Hunter shook his head. "I was terrible to live with after that. I hate admitting it, but I was suicidal there for a while until Teresa convinced me it wasn't the end of the world. At least my shoulder's healed enough for me to go into police work. How about you? I heard you were quite a wrestler."

"I won some international tournaments," Luke answered. "But, I couldn't eat my trophies and I had to find a way to pay the rent. I'll tell you this much, I don't miss being exhausted all the time."

"How come you didn't do something with literature instead of becoming a cop?" Hunter asked.

"There's never an easy answer to a question like that. I like helping people but I'm not cut out to be a teacher and I figured police work would give me something to write about." Luke took a sip from his soda. "It's too bad the money sucks."

"No money," Hunter said, putting his napkin on the table. "Man, tell me about it. There were times we were so broke I thought Teresa and I'd turn into Velveeta and saltines."

"I heard your parents are pretty well off. Weren't they willing to help out?" Luke asked.

"My dad wouldn't go out of his way to do anything for his kids."

A sudden arrival at their table together with Hunter's tone put an end to that topic.

# 30

HARTSON NUDGED HUNTER FURTHER INTO THE BOOTH AND, as he sat, immediately noticed the tension. "Am I interrupting something here?" he asked as he surveyed both of the younger officers. "You didn't tell him about Denny did you? I thought we agreed we'd talk to him about that together."

"What's Denny got to do with anything?" Luke asked. It seemed he couldn't avoid hearing about his roommate causing trouble even if Denny wasn't with the department any more. He shot Hartson an angry look. "Is this why you asked me to ride with you, so you could lay some crap on me about Denny?"

"It's not really Denny so much as the rape series up here that I wanted to talk to you about," Hartson said. "I just told the guys at Sex Crimes you might have some personal insight that could be helpful.

"That doesn't make any sense." Luke glared back and forth between Hartson and Hunter trying to silently communicate his disbelief. "Neither does having an audience for this conversation." Luke was beginning to understand why Hunter had been so nervous over the course of the last few minutes. He'd been expecting Hartson to show up and was under orders not to say anything about what was going on. Luke's square jaws clenched, spreading his lips into a tight line. This alleged confabulation was taking on the air of an ambush.

"Denny may be in a lot of trouble and I wanted you to know so you don't get blind-sided," Hartson said.

Luke gritted his teeth.

Hartson cleared his throat. "So you haven't told him anything about Denny?" he asked Hunter.

"We were talking about something else entirely." The tone of Hunter's answer did nothing to reduce the discomfort.

Some silences among friends are awkward, but this one that followed shaped up as a doozy and Luke decided he wasn't the one who'd slam the brakes on the accelerating tension.

Hartson pressed forward, deciding not to ask any more questions about the situation he'd walked in on.

"Sex Crimes asked Dr. Pantages to do a psychological work up on the suspect," Hartson continued.

Why would Denny's name pop up in relation to the rape series? The whole situation was starting to stink. Luke shifted in the booth and pointed his feet towards the door. His mind might not have known it, but his body wanted to run for the exit.

"You remember that the rapist doesn't say much?" Hartson continued.

Luke nodded. "And what does that tell us?" he asked.

"Dr. Pantages thinks that the rapist's controlling his victims and getting his rocks off is no longer enough to satisfy his compulsions."

Luke fidgeted. "Are you going to get to the part about the silent suspect and how that relates to Denny anytime soon?" he asked.

"I'm coming to that," Hartson said. "We know that the guy is trim to muscular, tall and in good shape." Hartson held up his hands to stave off Luke's next question. "I get that it's not much to go on especially since nobody's seen his face. But the victims all get examined by a doctor who preserves any physical evidence with the rape kit. We've recovered a pubic hair that tells us the suspect is either Black or part Hispanic and the semen indicates that he's Denny's blood type."

"That's not much to go on," Luke said.

"Dr. Pantages read all the case reports and sat in on some of the victim interviews. She's going to the divisional supervisor's meetings with some interesting insights. One of those insights is that the suspect deliberately doesn't say much so that his voice can't be used for any type of identification."

Luke reached up and massaged the knotting muscles at the back of his neck as the waitress interrupted to take Hartson's order of spaghetti and meatballs.

Hartson resumed his narrative as she walked away.

"Dr. Pantages feels that a serial rapist like this is likely to lead a Jekyll, Hyde kind of life and could work his way through dozens of victims before he gets caught. She also stressed that the need for sex isn't a motivation. In fact, this guy's likely to get all the sex he wants. He can probably con people and get most of what he wants in life simply by being charming. He's probably been around drug and alcohol abuse in his childhood but doesn't abuse them himself yet, and most likely can hide the impact they've had on his life."

"Are you saying this in some way applies to Denny?" Luke asked.

"You tell me," Hartson said.

Luke shook his head vigorously.

"How about the way he treats women?" Hartson asked. "Pantages says the ladies in the real world are likely to think he's really something. But that's not the most interesting part."

"If that's the best you've got, it doesn't convince me of anything," Luke said.

Hunter shifted his weight uncomfortably. Luke could almost feel sorry for him if he hadn't been part of this setup.

"Pantages thinks the guy has a law enforcement background," Hartson said.

"So, it's got to be Denny?" Luke asked.

"She's been struck by the victims' descriptions and the rapist's situational awareness. One victim said he stands with his left foot ahead of the right. We all know that sounds a lot like a field interview stance."

Hartson paused when his food arrived.

"Even if she's right, there are lots of guys with past and present cop experience," Luke said. He looked toward Hunter for a little support but his academy mate seemed more intent on studying the red and white checks on the tablecloth than in taking sides.

"That's just a couple pieces of Dr. Pantages' puzzle," Hartson responded. "She really seemed to focus on the way the suspect holds his flashlight. He keeps it away from his body the way we're taught at the academy."

Hartson shoveled a forkful of spaghetti into his mouth and looked up from his plate. "Think of what the guy does to avoid leaving evidence behind. He doesn't say much so we got next to nothing there. He covers his face with a ski mask, wears gloves and never takes his clothes off."

"The good news is that you've managed to get something to go on," Luke said. "The bad news is you'd be wasting your time focusing on Denny."

Luke glanced at Hunter. "And you still haven't told me what Hunter's doing here."

"Look," Hartson said. "We want to be wrong about the law enforcement angle. But in using it, Denny's name came up almost immediately."

"Is his the only name on the list?" Luke asked the question with the suspicion the answer might also explain what Hunter was doing there.

"I took the information to lineup and one of my officers named him as a possibility. He thinks Denny might keep his talking to a minimum to minimize the impact of his accent." Hartson poked a meatball towards Hunter. "Hank here agreed that the description fit Denny, so I asked him to come along to provide another friendly face when I filled you in."

Hunter looked away as Luke stared him down and Hartson continued.

Luke crossed his arms and waited, feeling the pizza turn to cement in his stomach.

"Don't forget the way he treats women," Hartson said.

"You're kidding, right?" Luke responded. "Denny has sex with women all the time because they like the way he treats them."

"You're making my point for me," Hartson went on. "Pantages says serial rapists often engage in more sex than you or I could handle. Besides you can't be sure he comes home every night. Not on the schedule you're working now. You're usually out on patrol when these rapes happen."

Luke was set to fire off a protest, but Hartson held his hands up to cut him off. Luke knew Hartson well enough to understand that he was doing it to protect him from saying something stupid but it still totally pissed him off.

"He may be charming to the ladies but think how he talks about women to us guys," Hartson continued. "He acts like a woman is just his next piece of tail instead of a human being. Add his physical description to his police service together with his spoken accent and he's a total fit for the probable rapist."

"You're wrong about this," Luke said. "There must be hundreds of guys with law enforcement backgrounds who match your non-description as well as Denny does."

"There's something I haven't mentioned yet," Hartson answered. "According to Dr. Pantages, a serial rapist's triggering event is likely to be a major disappointment in his life. It could be that his forced departure from the department caused some sort of psychotic break."

"Are you kidding me? A psychotic break? What about the background investigation we all went through just a few months ago." Luke pointed a finger toward Hunter to include him in his assertion. "And don't you think I'd notice some sort of change in Denny's behavior?"

Hartson stabbed at his spaghetti. "Remember what Dr. Pantages said, that these guys are Jekyll and Hyde types. Think about how careful the rapist is. If it's Denny, maybe he's just as careful when he's around you."

Luke bit his lower lip. "I can't listen to this anymore," he told Hartson. "You're just flat wrong. There's no way that it's Denny and I can't believe you asked me to give up my night off just to sandbag me like I'm some kind of moron."

"I'm sorry this pissed you off," Hartson said. "I'm just trying to prepare you for the worst." He turned to Hunter. "Thanks for your contribution to this. That's some kind of back up you provided."

"I thought you just wanted me here for moral support," Hunter said.

# 31

LUKE LET HIMSELF INTO NORTHERN DIVISION'S BACK DOOR the next day as second watch lineup finished and bumped into Hank Hunter who was emerging from the locker room ready to start his shift.

"Does the Sarge know you're coming?" Hunter asked.

"I told him I was going to drop by for a few minutes. Why, does that matter?" Luke asked.

Hunter chuckled. "Sorry," he said. "I always manage to find some way to stick my nose into other people's business. I asked because he mentioned he's got a ride-along tonight and I'm not sure what time she's arriving."

"A woman," Luke said. "It's about time he started getting a little female companionship again. I know it was hard on him when his wife left him when he came out here from Chicago. Do you know who she is?"

"Just the fact that it's a woman and that he's known her for a while," Hunter said. "He didn't seem to want to talk about it much. Listen, I wanted to apologize for my part in ambushing you last night. The Sarge was insistent that I be there when he told you about Denny and ordered me not to say anything before he arrived. I really felt like shit for the way it played out."

"Apology seems to be the theme of the evening," Luke said. "I'm here to tell T.D. that I overreacted and to apologize for being such a prickly S.O.B. I think my career would go a lot smoother if I had some of your people skills."

"I don't know about all that," Hunter said. "But I usually do a pretty good job of keeping my mouth shut."

Hunter set his equipment bag down and extended his hand. "We're both new at this cop business and we've a lot to learn. Still friends?" Hunter asked as the two shook hands.

"I can't go around losing any more friends," Luke said. "Give me a call the next time your wife's out of town and we'll grab a beer."

"Yes," Hunter said. "I'll be in touch about that soon. Right now, I'd better get out to my beat. I hear they've already got quite a few calls stacked."

Hartson rounded into the hallway from his office as the two rookies parted ways. He stole a quick glance toward his watch. "I've only got a few minutes," he told Luke. "Listen, I'm sorry about the way our conversation shook out with Hunter last night. I genuinely thought you might like having a friend around when you heard the bad news."

"I wouldn't call it news," Luke insisted. "Besides, you're more of a friend than Hunter is. I don't know him all that well."

"Anyway," Hartson said as he looked at his watch again.

Luke was smart enough to know when he was being dismissed, but he still had a couple things to say. "I just came to apologize about flying off the handle last night and to tell you not to take any of that stuff you heard about Denny too seriously. I don't know who said any of that stuff but I'd call it the ravings of a callow mind."

Hartson blinked. "What in the world does that mean?" he asked.

Luke chuckled. "Oops, there I go again. Whoever named Denny as a potential suspect in the rape series obviously has an immature mind. You mentioned that the idea came from one of your squad members. Who in the world was that?"

Hartson's stammering response indicated that the question caught him by surprise. "I, uh, well I uh, don't think telling you that's such a good idea. You've got enough problems with peer relationships without me adding to them."

This was not the type of response that Luke expected from Hartson who always spoke the truth and defended Luke, and even Denny, against anyone who spoke ill of them. "Are you saying you won't tell me?" Luke asked.

"Look, Luke," Hartson said. "I'm in a bit of hurry. Let's talk about this thing another time. For now, just believe me when I tell you you're better off not knowing."

Anger alerts started sounding in Luke's head. What good was his alleged friendship with Hartson if the man wasn't willing to treat him like a friend? Luke was sure Hartson sneaked another quick glance at his watch. It was a dismissive move but he decided not to be derailed from his original mission. "OK" he said. "Let's drop it for now. I know you were just looking out for me and somehow I still managed to act like you were the source of my problems."

"Don't sweat it," Hartson said. "I know what I had to say was a shock. I really hope this all works out for the best for your friend Denny." Hartson took a longer look at his watch.

"I'd better get going," Luke said. "I can see you're in a hurry."

Hartson's face took on a blush. "It's just that I've got this appointment is all."

"Wow," Luke said. "I never thought I'd see you so embarrassed about having a female ride-along."

"How did you know?" Hartson asked.

"You're not the only one with sources," Luke said, standing deliberately still and silent, waiting for Hartson's response.

"I've got a few things to wrap up in the office before I hit the field," Hartson said. "I'd better get back to it."

And that was that. Luke walked out the way he'd come in and started up his rickety Mercury. As he pulled out of the parking lot and turned west onto Eastgate Mall, he passed a Toyota Camry as it turned into the parking lot. The driver was a short-haired woman who Luke thought looked familiar. He knew he'd seen her before but he just couldn't place where.

# 32

ALTHOUGH PLENTY BUSY, THE ONE-FIVE-THREE CLUB wasn't crowded like it sometimes was shortly after second watch wrapped up at 11:30 at night. Bob Fiedler waited in the booth for Luke who'd detoured to the restroom before stopping at the bar for their second round of beers.

Luke soon pushed the beers onto the table and settled into the booth to pick at the remains of the rolled tacos and guacamole. He sipped from his Corona. "If you don't mind, I'd like to hear more about your winning your job back through the civil service commission," he said.

"Why so curious?" Fiedler responded.

Luke tried to put an innocuous expression on his face.

"It doesn't matter," Fiedler said. "I think every cop should know my story to deter Browner and some of the brass from screwing with the foot soldiers. A couple years ago, I started managing some apartments to get the free rent and supplement my income a little bit. Laura was riding with me..." He looked up from his beer. "You haven't met my girlfriend yet, have you?"

Luke shook his head.

"We'll all have to get together soon," Fiedler said. "We managed twenty-seven apartments in El Cajon, along with a few units on 48th Street, and some others on Marlborough a few buildings north of University Avenue. Dispatch advised me about a phone call from one of the tenants in the Marlborough complex.

"I was in the process of evicting a couple in an upstairs unit for failure to pay rent. They'd called me earlier that day to say they were done with their move, which, I might add, was a big relief to me since I didn't have to go over and check the property until I got off work the following morning.

"Dispatch told me to call the people living beneath the vacated apartment. It turned out they'd tried to reach me at home, but got no answer since I was either asleep or at work when they called.

"When I called the guy back, he told me that water was flowing into his place from upstairs and that he was worried his ceiling might collapse. I drove over and crawled through a window into the upstairs apartment. Once in, I discovered the people I evicted had turned the water on in the bathroom, stuffed the sink with a towel and left the water running. It took about five minutes for me to temporarily fix the situation and Laura and I left right away. I was available for calls the whole time.

"There was significant damage inside the building, so I sued the evicted tenants in Small Claims Court. I testified about what had happened and so did the tenant in the downstairs unit. The evicted tenants countered with testimony that there was no water running when they left the apartment and they even produced sworn affidavits from a couple of friends who swore they'd helped with the move and that everything was fine when they all left the apartment earlier that day.

"That totally pissed me off since I knew that four people had lied under oath in a way that not only disrespected the judicial process, but also impugned my professional integrity. So, another officer and I interviewed the second lying couple to prove a case of perjury and to support the report I'd filed against the evicted couple. The lying, scum-sucking, deadbeat tenants retaliated by filing a Citizen's Complaint Form with the department.

"The CCF initiated an investigation that concluded I'd not only left my beat, but my division too. It's nothing I ever denied, but the sergeant conducting the investigation ranted on and on about the fact that I'd left the entire division, which, by the way, I'd done by less than half a city block. So, although the flooded building was technically out of my division, it was practically across the street from my beat. Most people can spit the distance between my northernmost beat boundary and where the damage to the apartment occurred."

Although the incident had happened more than a year ago, Fiedler started getting worked up. He shook his head in anger and disbelief. "I didn't go there for some bullshit reason. This guy's ceiling might have collapsed in the middle of the night and I was so close to my beat I could have responded to any call without any delay. I had my handi-talkie with me, for god's sakes." Fiedler gulped a swig of beer. "Do you know a sergeant named Bimbel?" he asked.

"Never heard the name," Luke said.

"Take a guess at his nickname."

"I have no idea."

"It's 'Pimple,' and it's perfect for him. But the name doesn't come from some stupid wags just being cruel. The guy truly is a Grade AAA, extra large, pus-filled zit.

"Anyway, Pimple conducted the investigation and stretched the truth enough to get me fired. He just kept rambling on about what a terrible violation I'd committed, how officers are never allowed to leave their patrol divisions for any reason. How I'd shirked my sworn duty as a peace officer of the city of San Diego by breaching the public trust. He said I deserved to be stripped of the uniform and badge that sym-bolized that trust." Fiedler drained the last of his beer and went to the bar for the next round.

"I obviously know the ending," Luke announced when Fiedler re-turned. "You got your job back, but what did the hearing officers say about your violation?"

Fiedler answered as soon as he set down the beers. "The hearing officers didn't quite say it as bluntly as it'll sound coming from me, but their ruling is one of the reasons Southeast Division's still pissed at me.

"They basically ruled that Sergeant Pimple was full of shit for firing an officer on the strength of a citizen's complaint with virtually no basis in fact. A technical violation of the type I'd committed should have been examined in the light in which it arose. Southeast should have taken the totality of the circumstances into account, including the fact that leaving my division was comprised of crossing the border by a distance equal to what a good high school shot putter could toss a sixteen pound ball. More importantly, they should've factored in the knowledge that the complainants and their cronies were scum-sucking, perjuring deadbeats who were pissed off they had to pay for damages they'd caused, and for the lies they'd obviously told under oath."

"Nice," Luke said.

"You know who helped me get my job back?"

Luke shook his head.

"Caroline Rood. As POA President at the time, she told me from the beginning that the termination had been a string of misjudgments and malicious miscalculations as to what the civil service commission would tolerate. She sat in on the hearings and communicated to the commissioners that, in a case like mine, any negative personnel actions should be limited to the most minor sanctions possible.

"She told me later that the hearing officers were so pissed that the department had fired me over such obvious bullshit, they blocked any potential lesser punishments."

"You said the ruling was one of the reasons Southeast is so pissed at you. Are there other reasons?"

"Sure, I've pissed a few people off over the years, but no more than a lot of guys have. The most powerful ones like Browner are mostly mad that I got my job back, which shoots down their inflated ideas of how powerful and important they are."

"I obviously know that rookies have to put up with a lot of that type of crap," Luke said. "But I had no idea it happened to you senior guys too."

"Oh, yeah," Fiedler said. "It has its roots in the rookie BS we all have to put up with. Small-minded people with even an iota of power like to mistreat their underlings who usually don't have the guts or the support to fight back. It's why so many senior guys hate people like you who'll stand up for your rights from the beginning. It's too bad that encountering people like you doesn't make them reconsider what their behavior says about them. Instead, they choose to believe that you're defiant and unruly and need to be put in your place."

Luke nodded knowingly, took a swig and headed to the bar for another round while wondering if he should ask Fiedler's advice about Denny.

# 33

OH GREAT, LUKE THOUGHT FROM HIS POST AT THE BAR, this asshole again. Maybe Fiedler could give him some pointers on how to handle guys like Dick Arenas. Luke turned his back to Arenas' looming presence near him in an effort to deny the senior officer's existence. With any luck, the big man wouldn't even notice him.

Arenas either didn't see Luke or started up his own version of the ignore him and maybe he'll go away game. Arenas quickly ordered a pitcher of Budweiser then took the path past the booth where Fiedler was sitting. He did notice Fiedler.

"How do you like central division?" he asked as he approached.

"Hey, Dick, it's OK. How's it treating you?" Fiedler said.

"Not too bad."

"I'm with a couple other guys that you probably know from Southeast. Why don't you join us if you're here by yourself?" Arenas said.

"Thanks," Fiedler said. "But I'm here with Luke Jones and I know you two don't get along."

"You're shittin' me?" Arenas said. "The guy's a punk."

"That's not my experience," Fiedler said. "You should consider giving him another chance."

"A rookie only gets one chance with me," Arenas said. "He called for backup when it was totally unnecessary. The fact that he couldn't handle himself sure confirmed the shit I've heard about him."

"What shit is that?" Fiedler asked.

"He thinks he's smarter than everyone else just because he knows some big words and all." Arenas started to walk away and stopped. "Oh, and he doesn't know his place."

"I hate to say it," Fiedler said. "But it sounds to me like you've been listening to the wrong people."

"Yeah?" Arenas said with genuine surprise in his tone.

"I'm just saying you should back off and try making up your own mind," Fiedler said.

"Oh, I do that all right," Arenas said.

"You usually do. That's why what you're saying doesn't sound like you, but whatever. I'm just saying, I've spent some time with him and he seems pretty sharp to me," Fiedler said.

"I gotta get these beers to the guys," Arenas said, turning.

"Just remember what it was like when you were a rookie and consider giving him a chance," Fiedler said.

"I'll beat him down if he doesn't toe the line with me. How's that for giving him a break?" Arenas asked as he walked away.

"It sounds like it would be a big mistake on your part," Fiedler said to his back.

# 34

LUKE CARRIED THE BEERS BACK TO THE TABLE, CONFIDENT he'd done the right thing a few days ago by telling Fiedler about Biletnikoff screwing Denny out of his job, but he still wasn't sure if he should bring up the subject of the rape series. He'd originally believed that Fiedler's guidance might be helpful in Denny's getting his P.D. job back. But now that Denny's job application appeared to be moving smoothly through the channels of the Sheriff's Office, it seemed like a good idea to limit the damage of the rape investigation by keeping the knowledge of it confined to as few people as possible.

The waitress soon showed up with a re-fill of the chips and salsa and a second order of rolled tacos and Luke handed Fiedler a beer as she set the food on to the table. "So there's this other topic I keep meaning to get back to. What's up with that 'I Got Ugly' insignia you wear next to your name tag?"

Fiedler took a long sip of beer before responding. "I've got to warn you. If you get me started talking about myself, I might never shut up."

"I can't be hanging out with law enforcement legends and not know how they made their bones," Luke said.

Fiedler's grin widened for a second before he spoke. "This went down last spring. An armed robbery series was happening in all parts of the county and just about every victim or witness detectives talked to described the suspect with 'disturbing eyes' and as being both "big" and "ugly." The robber had committed more than fifty cases and was built like a rugby player. He had a massive nose, apparently almost never washed his hair, and brandished a six-inch revolver that he pulled from his waistband and used to threaten the victims. He was so notoriously ugly that the robbery detectives decided he probably got that way by wearing a theatrical disguise and they started calling him, "Big Ugly."

"I heard about this in the Academy," Luke said. "The two things I remember were how ugly the suspect was and about the skills of the arresting officer."

Fiedler chuckled. "Like with most things related to cop work, my arrest involved more luck than skill. Anyway, the robberies started happening nearly every day and Robbery Division soon borrowed officers from patrol to field plain-clothes teams to catch the guy. Eventually, too many officers got deployed to supply us all with unmarked cars so the Chief authorized overtime and the use of our personal cars.

"In April, the ugly son-of-a-bitch robbed the Bob's Big Boy over at Sports Arena and Midway and the manager followed him to the parking lot. What she did was reckless and dangerous, but she ended up giving us the lead that broke the case.

"Ugly spotted the manager trailing along behind him and emptied his six-shooter in her direction. Needless to say, that pissed her off big time. She wanted him arrested something awful and was positive the getaway car was a black, Lincoln Mark IV.

"It was the best lead we'd had in the case and, for several days, cops and sheriff's deputies took down all the Black Mark IV's in the county at gun point. One guy got stopped so many times that Robbery issued a Department Order with the vehicle's plate and a description of the owner, telling everyone not to stop the guy again."

"Like I always say, sometimes life isn't always fair," Luke said.

Fiedler nodded in agreement. "I live out east and my commute to work takes me past westbound State Route # 94 and Spring Street.

One day, I noticed a black Chrysler Cordoba a couple cars ahead and to the right of me. The driver was ugly as sin with long, greasy hair, an obscenely huge nose, and a female passenger who looked as bizarre as he did. Figuring it was probably nothing, I jotted down the plate information just in case and continued on to work.

"The plate came back registered to a John Alfred Samson. I ran that name for a driver's license and came up with two guys in San Diego County. One guy lived in Rancho Bernardo and didn't have any sort of criminal record. The other one had a criminal record as long as your pants, including an arrest for armed robbery. I pulled his arrest jacket and found a black and white booking photo that showed a guy with a fat scar running through his eyebrow, greasy black hair, and a gigantic nose."

"No wonder some of the guys thought he'd been wearing a disguise," Luke said.

Fiedler nodded as he took another sip. "I took the photo to Robbery where about half-a-dozen detectives had gathered to plan the night's surveillance.

"How about letting me in on this thing?" I asked them. "They pretty much told me to go fuck myself and kept right on talking like I wasn't even standing there. At which point I told them they should make an exception under the circumstances and all but one of them told me to go away.

"That one asked what circumstances I was talking about. That's when I tore off a piece of Scotch tape from the dispenser and used it to tape the suspect's photo to my forehead. It was fun as hell seeing the shocked look on everybody's faces and the sergeant asked if I had the guy in custody.

"I told them I couldn't do all their work then explained how I'd located the photo. Their expressions lit up the room like fireflies light up the Ohio sky before the whole bunch started planning how to take him down.

"I asked if they'd changed their minds about letting me in on the arrest and, suddenly I was the red hot movie star walking down the red carpet. I could've asked for anything I wanted and they would have given it to me.

"I told them I needed to hurry and put my uniform on so I wouldn't be late for line-up and the sergeant said he wanted me working plain clothes with one of his detectives. Not long after going into service I saw the black Cordoba accelerating onto 94 eastbound from 1500 "E" Street.

"The detective put the car's information out over the air and I accelerated like hell to try and catch up. Several more units moved into the area, but none of us was able to spot the car.

"I gave up and headed toward the guy's address. I eventually got off the freeway at Kelton Road before turning onto Bayview Heights Road and following it until it turns into Federal Boulevard. That's where I saw the Cordoba again. It was driving straight toward me but then it turned in at the parking lot of his apartment complex that was already infamous for non-stop drug dealing.

"I told dispatch and made a U-turn, all the time worrying the guy could be setting an ambush. It was about then that I saw the stopped Cordoba. No one was near it and the driver's door was wide open.

"Pretty soon, I saw his female passenger from earlier in the day. There was no mistaking her orange hair or the pinkish hue of her sweater. Trust me when I say this. Nothing approaching either of those two colors appears in nature anywhere. I thought the two of them had to be victims of some sort of bizarre love god bent on vengeance. She walked straight to the car and started sliding into the driver's seat. But Big Ugly was nowhere to be found.

"I kept a close eye on the car in case the ugly guy was waiting in ambush. The whole set up looked a little too phony and dangerous so, I drove out of the parking lot until I noticed a safe place I could pull into completely out of the Cordoba's line of sight. Several cover units arrived about that time and a couple guys wanted to rush in and make the take down. The robbery detective and I recommended that we set up a perimeter and get ready for a hot stop a couple blocks away since the two weirdoes in the car might not have any idea of our interest. A few hot shots insisted that we take her down right away so she could lead us to him before he got away.

"I told them that if she refused, we'd have blown any chance to use her to our advantage. Sergeant Pimple showed up and said the mere fact that I'd spotted the guy, didn't give me the right to run the whole show.

"I told him I wasn't trying to run anything that I was just trying to take the guy into custody without anyone getting hurt.

"This really pissed Pimple off for some reason I still can't figure out. I couldn't even fathom what he was talking about. How do you talk to a crazy person when time is short and people's lives are on the line?" Fiedler shook his head and took another swig of beer. "I said it was a bad idea to assume that the guy was spooked already and that if he wasn't, didn't my suggestions make a lot of sense?

"By that time, I was sure everyone had agreed to do it my way but, when the Cordoba started exiting the driveway, Pimple turned his overheads on in full sight of the apartments without giving any of us any warning.

"He made the stop while the rest of us were running to our cars and, sure enough, the suspect wasn't in the car. I was fuming. About that time, a civilian came up to ask if we were looking for someone and told us he'd seen an adult male acting suspicious a few blocks to the west. He put the pieces together when he saw us and figured the guy might be trying to escape. A couple of the more outspoken hotshots put the guy in their car and went to look for the bad guy.

"It turned out the tip was wrong because a teenager soon rode up on his ten-speed to say he'd been watching us from Emerald Hills Park on the other side of the freeway. He also said he'd been watching a big guy with greasy hair slinking along a fence at the bottom of the hill near the freeway. The whole thing seemed a little creepy to the kid and he thought we should know about it.

"I put the details over the air and the kid led us to the top of a hill with a good view to the bottom of the park. From there, I directed several responding units how best to surround the guy and the rest of us fanned out to form a perimeter. I have no idea why, but the whole thing pissed Pimple off to the point that he trumped up a bunch of phony charges and terminated me over the flooding incident." Fiedler shook his head, "And here I thought I was just out trying to catch the bad guys and protect the good guys. I still can't figure out what I did to piss him off.

"Anyway, once Big Ugly saw there was no way to get away, he turned himself in without any resistance. The subsequent investigation revealed that his lady friend was an accomplice in several of the robberies, so we arrested her too.

"Neither one of them would give anything up under interrogation so I suggested putting them together in a car along with a tape recorder that we'd stash under the front seat. For some reason, that suggestion turned out to be controversial as well because some of the patrol hotshots and my sergeant said it was a stupid idea and a waste of time. Fortunately, the ADA assigned to the case showed up and suggested that we at least provide the crooks with the opportunity to be stupid.

"When we listened to the tape later we discovered they'd found some way to scrape something against the cage in an effort to try and cover up what they said. They did manage to screw up the quality of the tape but we made out enough of what they said to convict them both on numerous counts of armed robbery.

"Not only that, Robbery held multiple live lineups in front of more than a hundred witnesses. Almost every one of them identified Big Ugly as the culprit. The toughest part of arranging those lineups was the requirement to repeatedly bring back the other big-nosed homely guys to fill out the line-up and provide a little challenge for the witnesses.

"And that whole process really pissed those guys off too. At first, because they had to miss so much work, and later because it dawned on them they'd been selected for being tall, dark, and ugly. It may not have been funny to them, but the thought of that select group looking so much like a notoriously ugly guy was absolutely hilarious to me.

"Anyway, the infamous Big Ugly was well and truly identified. The D.A.'s office charged him with all the armed robberies in the series and the two of them copped to everything after the public defender played them the recording.

"Chief Coleman personally gave me an Exceptional Performance Citation that my lieutenant prepared. Captain Whitley gave me four discretionary days off with full pay. I celebrated by having the 'I got UGLY' insignia made at the uniform shop and Chief Coleman said I could wear it for a year."

# 35

NEARLY EVERYONE ASSIGNED TO CENTRAL DIVISION'S SECOND watch patrol shift was in the report room at the end of shift except for Biletnikoff or any of his fellow sergeants. Luke had just finished a complicated report describing how he'd developed probable cause and arrested a notorious downtown druggie for violating 11550 of the California Health and Safety Code, being under the influence of a controlled substance, and needed a supervisor's signature at the bottom of the report before he could secure for the night.

Holding a mug of coffee, Dick Arenas soon appeared at the doorway before taking a seat at the duty sergeant's desk. Although Biletnikoff had conducted line-up at the beginning of the shift, Arenas was now clearly the acting sergeant and the situation created a rare and improbable conundrum where Luke actually would have preferred dealing with his real sergeant. Arenas actively hated Luke's guts and took advantage of every opportunity to show his animosity.

Luke considered searching out a supervisor just coming in to work for the approval signature, but decided he'd use the opportunity to try and clear the air. He stood in front of Arenas waiting for him to acknowledge his presence and receive the report. After several seconds it was obvious that Arenas knew Luke was there but was using the opportunity to display his sense of superiority in the hopes of forcing another public confrontation.

Arenas re-filled the stapler and rearranged a dozen or so pens according to size and ink color. But it wasn't until he reached up to adjust the knot in his tie that Luke's resolution to make nice with the fool evaporated. He dropped his lengthy report next to Arenas' coffee mug which interrupted the self-declared big shot's new task of neatly stacking blank report forms on the desktop.

Apparently annoyed at his ploy's lack of success, Arenas finally looked up, his expression devoid of any effort to hide his animosity. "Let me see," he said as he selected a red pen from the desktop before clicking the point open. "I think this should be adequate." Openly displaying an arrogant smirk, he lowered the pen toward the report.

Luke snatched the form away before Arenas could leave an ostentatious red mark.

"It doesn't need any editing," he insisted.

"Give me that back," Arenas said. "I'm acting sergeant and you're nothing but a wanna-be know-it-all rookie who wouldn't recognize a decent report if it bit him in the ass." He held out his hand with his palm held up. "I don't care what anybody says, you're a loud-mouthed punk who doesn't know his place and you'd better give that report back."

This was more than Fiedler could tolerate and he stood from his chair in the corner. "Leave off, Arenas."

The nearly palpable disdain Arenas held toward Fiedler because of his support for Luke colored his raspy voice. "Mind your own business and shut the fuck up." Then he turned his attention back to Luke. "I've got more than twelve years on this department. What gives you the right to challenge me about what is or isn't in a good police report?"

"For one thing, I've got actual knowledge of how to write, which I'm pretty sure trumps your departmental longevity," Luke shot back.

Fiedler inserted his opinion. "Luke's got a Master's Degree in literature. What have you got other than a big mouth?"

Arenas shoved his chair back abruptly to stand away from the table. Keeping his gaze trained on Luke, he spoke to Fiedler. "You'll stay out of this if you know what's good for you."

"No way, I'm staying out of anything," Fiedler responded. "Luke knows what he's doing and he doesn't need you messing up his work."

Unable to restrain his rage, Arenas exaggeratedly sucked in his gut which pushed his chest out like King Syndicate cartoonists used to puff out the torso of Bluto, Popeye's arch-nemesis. "Like you'd have some way of knowing." Arenas paused a few seconds, his muscular tautness visibly trumpeting his building anger. "Why don't you go ahead and show us your report writing awards?"

Fiedler opened his mouth to speak, but Arenas beat him to the punch.

"You used to have guts, but now you suck up to this punk ass recruit just because he killed that scroat at the Golden West a while ago. Now you're nothing more than a joke that sucks up to a punk ass rookie who doesn't respect anybody or anything."

# 36

"Get out of his face," Luke demanded.

"Let me explain a few things to you two clowns," Arenas shouted. "As the acting sergeant, I'm your supervisor and both of you need to behave accordingly."

"I don't think so," Luke said. "To me, you're just another guy on the squad with a coffee cup and a false sense of self-importance."

"You'll hand that report over right now, or I'll…"

Luke could barely control his disgust. "You'll what? Not cover me when I call for it?" He gave Arenas a second to respond, but the silence was met only with more pronounced puffing of the chest.

Luke stalked out of the room in search of a real supervisor and found Lt. Rood in her office. She invited him in, asked him to sit, and started reading as Luke sized up the surroundings that clearly indicated the lieutenant's pride in her academic and professional accomplishments. Her framed police academy graduation certificate drew his attention before he took in her college degree, her sergeant's certificate, more than a dozen framed commendations and her lieutenant's certificate.

Several framed photos also stood out. There was one of her shaking hands with the previous chief when being promoted to sergeant, another showed her receiving a commendation from Chief Coleman and still another showed her decked out in an elegant grey suit as she stood at a lectern with the POA plaque displayed on the front.

"This is one of the best reports I've ever seen," she told Luke. "That drug expertise you laid out establishing probable cause for the arrest is tricky stuff and you pulled it off beautifully." She handed Luke the report. "Keep up the good work."

"Thank you lieutenant," Luke said.

"There's something I'd like to ask you before you go," Rood said. "Your transfer request to Northern Division crossed my desk a few days ago. Do you mind me asking why you want to make a change so early in your career?"

Luke settled back in the chair, wondering if he should speak the truth about his intolerance for Biletnikoff and his rookie-baiting cronies. There was also the possibility that the animosity his sergeant held toward him might result in Biletnikoff's recommending that Luke fail probation at the end of his first two years. Hartson had been an effective buffer between the two of them but, with Hartson now gone, Luke's line of defense was clearly compromised.

He knew he needed a seasoned officer as a mentor, someone to whom he could speak the unvarnished truth and receive wise counsel in return. He was confident that Fiedler would fit that role if his transfer didn't go through which made him decide then and there not to ask Fiedler's advice about the rape nonsense. There was no sense trying to help one friend out while putting another in jeopardy at the same time.

Luke was pretty sure he could trust his new lieutenant but decided to keep his thoughts and motivations for the transfer close to the vest. "Sgt. Hartson was my FTO," Luke said. "He's got a lot to teach. I admire his quiet leadership and think I could benefit by continuing to work with him."

"Sounds reasonable enough," Rood said. "But these requests take time. I'll see what I can do to make it happen by shift change."

"That would be great," Luke said. "Thanks, lieutenant."

There was a new energy and noticeable purpose in Luke's step as he walked toward the report room. Once inside, he headed for the sergeant's desk intent on dropping the report in front of the still huffing Arenas, but the acting sergeant made it impossible for him to execute his plan.

Arenas stuck out his hand. "That report still needs my approval," he said. "Give it back to me so I can have a look."

"No thanks," Luke said. "It's already been approved." He held the report up to display the lieutenant's signature.

"You can't do that," Arenas bellowed. "That's bullshit."

"Lieutenant Rood said it was an excellent report," Luke told him as he held the pristine pages up for Arenas to examine. "She didn't see a need to correct anything."

"So, first you had Fiedler running interference for you and, when that didn't work, you went running to the lead girl-dog for protection?" Arenas said. "I was right about you Jones. You're nothing but a big-mouth who should remember there won't always be punks and other girls around for you to hide behind."

Luke heard a subtle chuckle behind him coming from several people. He and Arenas must have been putting on quite a show and he knew that his insubordinate antics might genuinely be putting his career in jeopardy.

The laughter should have been sufficient to check his conduct. But he'd ignored his instincts for too long to suddenly kowtow to the behaviors of petty people with Napoleonic complexes. The time had come for Arenas to understand the consequences of pointlessly screwing with Luke Jones.

"This coming from a coward who's afraid of a couple cowboys with knives," Luke said. "If I weren't so sure you were joking, I'd point out that your alleged bravery spikes exponentially when no armed suspects are around."

"What the fuck're you talking about?" Arenas shouted as he stood away from the table. "You're the one who called for cover…"

Luke counterbalanced Arenas' explosive fury with a moment of steady silence before he spoke. "You may forget your acts of cowardice, but I don't when they directly affect me," Luke said. "I'm talking about the line of crap you handed me the night I called for cover when Shimmer and I contacted two potential robbery suspects armed with knives. You said you'd never cover me again because it was chicken-shit to ask for cover under those circumstances."

Eyes collectively swung toward Arenas to take in his response.

"As I recall, Rookie, you called for help because their knives scared you."

The unanimous audience swung back in Luke's direction.

"Believe what you choose," Luke answered. "But I'll tell you one thing that'll last from now until the devil catches a chill in hell. I'm through with your cowardly posturing at my expense and I won't tolerate your screwing with my friends. I'm one rookie you don't want to mess with and you'll cover me whenever I ask for cover. I don't know how to say it any plainer than that."

"Oh, yeah?"

With Arenas' "oh, yeah" failing to meet the standard of a zippy comeback, the tension in the room dissipated noticeably. But Luke's next response was worth a short wait.

"Bravery is silent and elegant," he said. "Bravado is blustery and ostentatious. You're the king when it comes to bravado and a guttersnipe when it comes to bravery. You will cover me or anybody in this room when we ask for it, or I'll kick your ass." Luke shuffled forward a couple feet toward Arenas to punctuate his point.

The air in the room filled briefly with expectation as Arenas looked around for support. When he couldn't find any, he shrank back into his chair looking like he wanted to disappear.

Luke took a quick look around the room. Fiedler had already gone. He leaned menacingly toward the adversary who'd gone out of his way to pick a fight before walking abruptly from the room.

# 37

LUKE FOUND HIS MIND WANDERING DURING LINEUP after another night of fitful sleep but he tuned in just enough to ascertain that there was nothing going on that needed his undivided attention. He amused himself by taking in his surroundings and checking out his fellow officers. Devree projected an aura that was aloof and engaged at the same time and left Luke wondering yet again how he could pull that off. He was a personable guy who managed to stay out of trouble and get along with nearly everyone while steadfastly refusing to take anyone's shit. The caper with the spoiled brats and their balloons was a good example. It was almost a certainty that, if Luke had been the one who hurled the water missiles at those young punks, he'd be looking for another job. Not Devree. No one even filed a complaint in spite of the threats from the teens to the contrary. Luke wondered if the three boys had told their parents and been suitably punished or if they'd decided that discretion was the better part of valor and made up a story about how the inside of the car got soaked.

A few seats away, Shimmer sat slumped in his chair. He was on light duty and assigned to a desk because of his fractured hand that the doctor had described as a "boxer's fracture" to the fourth metacarpal. The blackened circles under his eyes had taken on a permanent look and Luke decided that he'd begin to look the same way if he didn't start getting a little sleep. No one was more surprised than Luke that the little guy had turned out to be a pretty good pal. After Nadine Brown had pulled Luke aside and mentioned the loss of Shimmer's son, he'd made it his business to learn the story. Luke remembered Hartson had once told him to cut Shimmer some slack, so it was to Hartson he'd turned for more information.

The three-year-old had drowned in the backyard pool while Shimmer was at work. His wife Beverly had gone into the house for just a minute to get some iced tea. Then the phone rang. The conversation with her brother had lasted a little longer than expected and Shimmer's son fell into the pool when he tried to retrieve a soccer ball. There was no hope by the time Shimmer's wife reached him. Shimmer blamed her and she blamed herself and Shimmer couldn't keep his hands off the bottle after it happened.

After hearing the details of the drowning, Luke learned more about the time Shimmer had killed a guy when trying to save a woman's life. Only he didn't save her life. Luke thought about what might help him if he'd suffered those circumstances and the answer was--nothing. Luke had no idea what to do for him because there was no help for what Shimmer had gone through. All he could do was to continue to be the man's friend to the best of his ability. Fortunately, Shimmer made that easy since he still treated Luke like a hero for saving his life.

Arenas sat opposite Shimmer and scratched out a few notes while Biletnikoff blathered on. For the life of him, Luke couldn't imagine what he could be writing. There were no detailed reports on anything, no APBs, no BOLOs, no descriptions of suspects and not even a partial license plate that needed to be remembered.

Sgt. Biletnikoff's droning voice finally fully penetrated Luke's reverie, "I have a special recognition for Dick Arenas this evening for his handling of that drug bust down on Fifth and "F" streets a couple weeks ago. He wrapped up a couple of the major players down here and the A.D.A called to say they both copped out and will serve a good stretch in the pen. That was fine work, Dick."

A tepid applause followed the announcement until Deputy Chief Browner made his way into the room. "We've got a special presentation today," Biletnikoff said after the shock of the Chief's arrival had subsided. "Officer Shimmer here did some outstanding work the other day and found an old woman who'd walked away from a rest home and was close to death. Chief Browner, would you like to do the honors?"

Browner replaced Biletnikoff at the lectern and announced that he was there to present Shimmer with a Commanding Officers' Citation for "almost certainly saving the life of a helpless old woman by utilizing advanced policing techniques and conducting a diligent search when other officers had given up."

Fiedler nudged Luke. "I told you there was something fishy going on up in the park that night. What do you suppose this is all about?" he asked.

Luke had no idea and signaled that with a shrug and a confused expression.

Once the hullaballoo about Shimmer's "extraordinary work" had subsided, Biletnikoff called Luke's name. "Jones you've got a request for a ride-along for tonight. Someone named Sibyl Vane. She'll be waiting for you at the front counter when we finish up here."

Luke wasn't sure he'd heard correctly. Sibyl here? Then the unsolicited chirping started.

"Hey Jones, you getting so famous you have women asking for you by name?"

"Don't drown the poor woman in ten-dollar words."

"Tell her she can ride with me if she wants to see how a real man does it."

Luke felt his face turning crimson as he wondered what had prompted her to ask to be his ride-along. As much as he'd wanted to see her again, he wasn't sure he was ready for her close-up scrutiny.

# 38

LUKE TOURED THE NORTH-SOUTH GRID OF THE Gaslamp Quarter, distracted by his gorgeous ride-along. Sibyl Vane looked better than he'd remembered, but her presence created an awkward tension. His mind kept flipping back to the way her body had felt as he held her on the dance floor. Then every time he hauled his mind back to the present, he worried that she'd find his work tedious and boring. They'd been together in the car for more than an hour and all he'd done so far was drive around and tell stories over the incessant chatter intruding from the police radio in the background.

At least it was a pleasure regaling her with tales from the Gaslamp Quarter's infamous past. And she did seem appreciative but, after all, she was an actress.

Geographically, the quarter was comprised of sixteen and a half blocks extending from Broadway on the north, to Harbor Drive on the south, and from Fourth Avenue on the west, to Sixth Avenue on the east. Originally called New Town, the Gaslamp now formed the core of San Diego's shabby downtown area after emerging as a solution to a problem created by the city's original European settlement a few miles to the north.

That original settlement, now known as Old Town, was anchored by a Spanish Presidio strategically placed on a hillside with panoramic views of the bay to the west, rolling hills to the north and a wide valley to the east. Unfortunately, the fortress mentality hadn't worked so efficiently in assisting with the inevitable civic expansion of a growing community since all necessary goods and stores had to be transported up the steep hill via horse and wagon.

Years later, William Heath Davis, a wealthy San Francisco businessman, initiated expansion of the New Town area when he purchased a hundred-sixty acres in 1850. His subsequent expansion, driven by his pumping ever more capital into the project, ultimately failed.

It took the arrival and participation of Alonzo Erastus Horton, another wealthy San Francisco-based investor, before New Town started living up to its promise. Horton's initial capital infusion consisted of the improbably low cost of just two-hundred-sixty-five dollars that he used to buy eight-hundred acres of land. He followed that investment with fifty-thousand dollars to build a wharf. He personally laid out the street grids, and selected the size and configuration of the building lots that he sold throughout the area. Horton also chose Fifth Avenue to be the main street within his ambitious downtown development area.

Having set the price of interior lots at one-hundred dollars, he charged one thousand dollars for corner lots. On March 24, 1869, Horton earned more than one-tenth of his investment back when he sold several lots for more than five-thousand dollars and numerous more modest lots for $100. New Town was underway.

"He sounds like quite a businessman," Sibyl contributed.

"Yes," Luke answered, "but he and William Heath Davis both died broke."

"That seems odd," Sibyl said. "How did that happen?"

"I don't know all the history," Luke said. "But, I suspect it was as simple as the cycle of wealth."

"The cycle of wealth?" Sibyl asked.

"Have you ever noticed that wealth is almost always generated by a small core of people?" Luke asked. "People who create wealth also frequently lose what they've created. I think it stems from their willingness to risk their fortunes on huge gambles. The risk, reward ratio doesn't always work out in their favor. Many of them seem to lose as frequently as they win, which can often be attributed to their being ahead of their time. The people necessary to help them achieve their goals don't share their vision or drive, and that reticence sometimes obstructs the process."

"There used to be a lot of foot traffic down here," Luke went on. "In the 1880s and '90s the Gaslamp Quarter turned into a red light district with saloons, gambling halls and bordellos. The sailors stationed here called it the Stingaree."

"There's a movie starring Irene Dunne called "Stingaree" that's about an Australian bandit and an opera singer," Sibyl said.

"I don't know where that title came from," Luke told her. "But, I do know that the name evolved down here from a saying that people were more likely to get stung by the people walking the streets than any bathers were to get stung by the stingrays in the bay.

"New Town's fame for adult entertainment kept increasing over the decades. Its forty thousand or so inhabitants could choose between more than seventy taverns that included the Old Tub of Blood, Legal Tender, and the First and Last Chance Saloon. The boom eventually dried up though and the ensuing bust left the area with a population of only about fifteen thousand people."

Luke pulled away from the curb, drove on, and parked at Horton Plaza. "It was a great honor for Alonzo Horton when they first chose the name. But now, Horton Plaza's seedier than Hades. It, and the surrounding area, is full of pornographic theatres, adult bookstores and happy-ending massage parlors. I guess the silver lining is that the whole district has been set aside for redevelopment. There's a plan in place to preserve the old buildings by offering tax incentives to wealthy investors. There's even talk about replacing the street lights with gas lamps."

"Make it a show place? Sounds like a smart plan," Sibyl said.

"I suppose so. The downside is that the Centre City Development Corporation is forcing longstanding, successful businesses to close. My favorite Chinese restaurant has already closed its doors."

"Why didn't they just relocate?"

"That sounds good in theory. But they couldn't find a place with comparable rent in an area where their customers would be likely to follow." Luke pointed to the Oyster Bar, a thriving restaurant in the Louis Bank of Commerce building on Fifth Avenue. "That used to be owned by Wyatt Earp. He once owned four saloons and gambling houses down here and made a lot of money."

"I didn't know Wyatt Earp ever lived in San Diego."

"For several years between his time in Arizona and Alaska. He died in Los Angeles in 1929."

"What an interesting place. Is the Gaslamp Quarter your usual beat?"

"It has been for the last few months. That's why I know all the stories—and just what a dump this place is."

"Are the crimes you deal with similar to what went on in the Stingaree?"

"I suppose so since I pick up a lot of public drunks and arrest folks for various crimes related to drugs and shoplifting, prostitution, street muggings and the occasional murder. But, some nights nothing much happens that comes to our attention. This is one of those nights so far, which makes it a good time for dinner if you're hungry."

# 39

"I'M ENJOYING THIS CHANCE TO GET TO KNOW YOU BETTER," Sibyl said before she took another bite of her grilled chicken. "That club was too noisy for any real conversation and I wanted to learn more about what you do."

"Sounds a little like getting to know your fellow characters by studying their lines in a play," Luke said. Her interest in understanding his job was both flattering and dangerous. What if she hated seeing him in action and bolted before they really got acquainted?

He hoped for the best, but had never experienced the greatest of luck with either love or loyalty.

Luke caught sight of a man shuffling down the sidewalk looking like he might trip over a crack at any moment. The gait put him in mind of the Professor, one of the ones worth saving that he hadn't been able to help. In one of his sober moments, the Professor, a notorious downtown drunk who had taught literature at UCLA and had an oddly accurate moral compass, had challenged Luke for the way he treated the homeless and the hungry. Luke understood that living up to the Professor's standards would make it impossible to survive as a police officer, but the Professor had drank himself to death before Luke could challenge the man's naïve assertions. He still missed the old guy, especially on nights like these when he felt as off balance as the drunk outside the window.

"You intrigue me," Sibyl said. "I can't remember meeting another man who could quote Jack London, Oscar Wilde and Shakespeare." She scooped a forkful of rice. "But I bet you hear that a lot."

"Mostly I just take a lot of crap about using big words, and my career choice, after studying literature."

"You'll have to tell me sometime how you chose police work. Me? I love a well-turned phrase whether its poetry, prose or lyrics."

"Me too. Speaking of music, do you know Michael Franks?"

"I love Michael Franks. Have you heard 'I Don't Know Why I'm So Happy I'm Sad?'" She started humming then softly sang the chorus.

Luke, who couldn't carry a note in a shoebox, joined in with the spoken word, "Your Laissez-faire, and your long chestnut hair, drive me crazy, make me lazy..."

Their eyes met and they both smiled. "He's from San Diego, you know," Luke said.

"I did not know that," Sibyl said as she stirred her iced tea with a straw. Her grin took on a seductive aspect.

Things just seemed to keep getting better with Sibyl, and the thought crossed Luke's mind that her idea to go on a ride-along hadn't been such a bad one after all.

"You know," Sibyl said, "the way great writers put words together is the biggest reason I love acting."

Luke nodded in agreement. "I know your mother's an actress. How much did that influence your love of the theater?"

"I suspect it's a huge influence. But I just don't know for sure because she kept pushing me into it. I guess it comes down to the old argument about the chicken or the egg."

"What parts has your mother played?"

"She's played a lot of great parts, but she spent most of her career with small theatre groups so she didn't get a lot of recognition. She landed a few movie parts, but usually got cast as a minor character who didn't even figure in the credits. What about your mother? How did she influence you?"

"I'm not sure how to answer that," Luke said. "I can't honestly say I ever really knew her. She got diagnosed with terminal cancer before I turned three, but didn't die until I was nineteen. My sister's the oldest of us kids and she was more of a mother to me than my real mom was."

"That sounds tough. Does your sister drive you crazy? I ask because my mom really pushes me to the edge sometimes."

"My sister's great. She does occasionally push, but she backs off when I give her the-you're doing the mom thing again-look."

"I wish I had an expression that would make my mother back off. She pushes me hard about the theater. I know she wants to succeed vicariously through me and that makes her keep pushing, but she never turns off the pressure and that drives me crazy. The worst part is that she can be a real sweetie when she decides to be, but it's always for someone else's benefit, not mine."

"How do you mean?"

"My first part at the Globe was Cordelia in *King Lear*. She brought a bunch of friends down from L.A., sent me flowers, treated us all to dinner after the show and wrote a rave review that was published in the *L.A. Times*. I know that sounds nice and all, but in the end, it was all about impressing her friends, not about supporting me."

"I've heard of worse things."

"The problem is that's the extent of the good stuff she does, showing me off like a trophy. And she can be perfectly awful. I almost quit acting altogether because of the way she hounded my high school director about giving me the female leads. I love her, but she never lets go of running my life."

"I get what you're saying. It sounds a lot like me and my dad."

Sibyl was on too much of a roll to be ready to listen for long. "She tells me what parts to try out for and never stops harping on my hair. Even though she pushes her role of stage mother to the max, she tells me I should stick with acting only long enough to find some man with a lot of money who'll marry and take care of me. In other words, I should do exactly what she did. And she constantly tries fixing me up on dates. If she knew some of the guys I've gone out with down here, she'd freak."

"Like policemen?"

"Police*man*," Sibyl corrected. "You're the only cop I've ever dated. And it's a bit of a stretch calling this a date, wouldn't you say?"

"Well, I know cops don't qualify on her wealthy list."

"I refuse to let my mother run my life," Sibyl said with emphasis between bites. She reached across the table and took Luke's hand.

# 40

THEIR SEAMLESS CONVERSATION CONTINUED IN THE squad car after dinner. "How are your two friends from the disco?" Sibyl asked.

"Denny's my roomie," Luke said. "I see him pretty much every day. He'd be doing fine if he'd give up his obsession with getting laid. He's pretty close to getting hired by the Sherriff's office. Maybe that will calm him down a bit."

"How about the married guy?" Sibyl asked.

"You mean Hank Hunter. Are you saying you don't know who he is?".

"Should I?"

"He's a local star."

"You mean he's an actor?"

"No, he used to play for the Padres until he injured his shoulder. One of the local TV stations has been profiling his police career since our first day in the academy."

"I guess I'm too new here to have heard of him," she said. "But I sure recognized how handsome he is."

"Ouch," Luke said. "I couldn't help but notice you approached him that night instead of me."

"He may be handsome but…"

"What? He lacks my magnetic personality?"

They both laughed.

"Well, not exactly, but--well, maybe I shouldn't say it..."

"Say what?"

"He's a friend of yours?"

"Sort of. I don't know him all that well. But, I do keep hearing he's the guy I should strive to be like. He's smart, athletic, happily married with a baby and he always says the right thing, but even more importantly, he knows when to keep his mouth shut. Oh, yeah, and I'm told he's good looking too."

"He certainly is that. But he seems pretty one dimensional to me. He can't seem to see beyond his family and his career. There's nothing wrong with having them as your focus, but I need someone who appreciates literature and the arts," she grinned. "Know anyone like that?"

Luke smiled back, genuinely charmed. "Denny's an interesting character, don't you think"?

"He is a character all right," Sibyl answered. "But, from what you've said, he's all about the disco and the bedroom."

Luke started to protest.

"Both of them fit in the category of being a lady's man."

"That's definitely true about Denny," Luke agreed. "But Hunter's completely faithful to his wife as far as I know."

"I guess I didn't say that right. What I meant to say is that I'll bet neither of them encounters many women who don't fall for their charms."

"How do you mean?" Luke said, intrigued by her savvy analysis.

"Have you seen "Star Wars"?"

Luke nodded.

"With Denny, it's like the Force is with him. His essence projects a joi de vivre that's exhibited through his love of women. It's mildly intriguing for an encounter or two, but ultimately, it's narrow and boring because it's motivated by something shallow and meaningless."

Luke nodded in agreement. "I can't argue with that. But that's not to say he doesn't fill up a room when he enters it."

"Yes. You do get it. Hank has the same type of charisma, but one of my girlfriends with me that night thought both of them were all good looks and charm and not much else."

Luke was surprised. "That sounds like a bit of a stretch. Everybody keeps telling me I ought to strive to be more like Hunter."

"I don't buy it," Sibyl said. "When you stood next to them the other night it was like I was watching two beams of light refracting off a solid column. You're the substance and they're the flash. I'm here because I trust you, and I wouldn't ask them to escort me across the street."

"You don't actually think they're dangerous?"

"All I'm saying is that if I were writing a play about the three of you, I'd make you the hero and they'd either be the bad guys or shiftless sidekicks."

"Do you dissect everyone you meet like that?"

"I do it a lot I'm afraid. It's a tool that I hope helps make me good at what I do.

A radio call about store employees detaining a combative petty theft suspect at the Palms Liquor Store at Fourth and Broadway interrupted their conversation. "It looks like our quiet night might be about over," Luke told her.

# 41

LUKE SIZED UP THE OWNER OF THE STORE WHO walked toward him. He was a perfect medium in every way, medium height, medium weight, had medium brown hair and brown eyes, was about forty years of age, and his face had no distinguishing features. Even his beige slacks and the tan shirt he wore were boring. It occurred to Luke that selling liquor in downtown San Diego to a clientele of needy and addicted people could wash away just about anyone's individuality.

Luke offered his hand and introduced Sibyl. He soon learned that the owner had seen the thief stick a bottle of Night Train wine under his jacket, had let him walk out of the store to establish the elements of the crime of petty theft, and arrested him with the help of two employees.

Luke opened the office door and handcuffed the suspect. He'd arrested the guy and his twin brother numerous times and knew that the ravages of alcohol and drugs had combined to make them both look several years older than their actual age. Robert Lancaster was a squashed up stump of a man.

Luke obtained the necessary report details from the owner, then steered Lancaster to the cage of the squad car. He introduced him to Sibyl as the three walked together.

As soon as he sat behind the wheel, Luke read Lancaster his rights and struck up an amiable conversation. "Remember, you don't have to talk to me," Luke said as soon as Lancaster started to spill his guts.

Lancaster nodded. "I remember," he said.

"I thought so," Luke answered. "Before we go any further, my parents taught me to always inquire after another person's health. With that in mind, I'm just asking, how are you doing tonight?"

"Well, other than being arrested and in need of a drink, I'm A-OK," Lancaster said.

Luke nodded and smiled. "Is that why you went in to the store looking for something to drink?"

"Yes."

"Everybody gets thirsty," Luke said. "What's your favorite drink?"

"Whatever's alcoholic and in front of me," Lancaster said.

Luke had arranged the rear-view mirror so he and Lancaster could see one another and checked it to make sure that his prisoner could see him before he smiled. "I know just how you feel. My favorite drink is really dry champagne."

"Wine's OK, but what I really like is Johnnie Walker," Lancaster responded.

"Johnnie Walker, now that's good stuff," Luke agreed.

"How about you, lady? Sorry, I forgot your name," Lancaster said.

"I'm Sibyl. I prefer white wine, but Johnnie Walker's OK too," Sibyl said.

"I noticed you didn't have any money on you when I checked your pockets in the store," Luke said. "How'd you intend to pay for the booze?"

"I just wanted a little taste of something and figured I'd pay the guy back one of these days, which is what I tried to tell the guy in the store, but he wouldn't listen."

"Do you have any sort of regular income?" Luke asked.

"Not really," Lancaster said. "But, I would've paid him back eventually. He'd have known if he'd listened. He could learn a lot from you. You listen, which is what most people don't do."

"I try to be a good listener," Luke said as he pulled into the station.

Once he parked the car, Luke checked to make sure Lancaster hadn't accrued any new warrants before transporting him to jail.

"Can I ask you a silly question," Sibyl inquired after the jail deposit.

"Sure."

"Are you that nice to everyone you arrest?"

"I'm not sure what you mean."

"You asked him how he was doing, what he liked to drink and reminded him he didn't have to talk to you. Do you do that with every crook you arrest?"

"I try to do it with nearly everyone. He was lucid, wasn't resisting and wasn't cussing me out. I've learned that being polite to people I arrest declares an interest in them as human beings which gets them to tell me not just what they did, but what they intended to do before they did it. Articulating that in my report can mean the difference between the suspects spending the night in jail or going to prison for several years."

"How?"

"More often than not, what they're willing to say depends on how they feel about the officer who arrests them. Take this guy for example. Because he told me he intended to steal the wine when he walked in, I charged him with burglary instead of petty theft, and his confession will most likely get him sentenced to three years in prison. If some other cop had arrested him and been rude and Mr. Lancaster had kept his mouth shut that might have saved him about three years of his life. So, by being nice to Mr. Lancaster, I most likely nudged him into the penitentiary for a few years."

Luke stopped talking and waited for Sibyl's criticism.

"Interesting," was all she said.

# 42

LUKE HEARD THE FRONT DOOR OPENING AND CLOSING followed by the sound of Denny's voice. Next came a young woman's giggling and the tinkling of ice clinking into glasses. Believing that he could relax now that Denny appeared to be home for the night, he turned his attention back to Fitzgerald's Tender is the Night.

Although it was well past midnight, Luke soon heard more muted giggling followed by the front door's opening and closing and the shower turning on at the opposite end of the apartment. When Denny brought a date home this late, he usually turned his salsa music on too loud and accompanied it with the percussion sounds of a headboard slapping against his bedroom wall until dawn. Tonight's sexual jam session had lasted less than an hour.

The abbreviated sexual liaison followed by a shower almost certainly signaled an imminent departure, so Luke carted his book to the living room to wait for Denny's bedroom door to open. He snatched up the shiny white disco suit Denny had crumpled up and tossed indiscriminately into a corner of the sofa and flipped it onto the easy chair.

Denny emerged a few minutes later with a pick-comb stuck in his wet hair. He flipped a black baseball cap in one hand, wore a matching sweatshirt and new Levis, carried his camera bag to the front door and set it down before sitting next to his suit. "I'm heading out to meet a lady friend for a photo shoot at the beach. You should come along," he said.

"No thanks," Luke said knowing it was a half-assed invitation since Denny couldn't possibly believe that he'd accept. "I've got other plans and besides, have you forgotten about the beach rapist?"

"Ah man, I can handle myself," Denny said. "And don't go reading the whole night away again. This is the time for romance."

"You just had sex with a woman you brought home from the disco and can't bear to stay in and get a good night's sleep because there's another woman hot for your body out there somewhere?" Luke said.

Denny's delight in Luke's inability to comprehend his drive for more sex made his face sparkle. "She was real good and helped me decide something," Denny said.

Luke gave him the obligatory prod, when he didn't continue with his point. "Yes?"

"I wanna see how many days in a row I can shank a different woman. And I've decided to celebrate by doing a photo shoot at the beach with one of my ladies. There's nothing wrong with that and you should come along for the fun."

"Shag," Luke said.

"What?"

"You mean shag, not shank."

"I said what I meant, homey. Of course, the ladies won't mind since it'll be an assault with a friendly weapon." Never one to employ subtlety, he asked Luke along for the third time and offered to have his "lady" bring a friend along.

"No thanks," Luke said.

"You gotta get laid more," Denny taunted.

Luke didn't respond.

"Be that way," Denny said. "But, that shouldn't stop you from helping me count the ladies I shag, should it?" He followed his statement with a huge grin, apparently proud that he'd managed to use both of their euphemisms for sex in one sentence. "By the way, that one," he tossed his head toward the door, "was number two, the first one was earlier today."

Luke stifled a chuckle. He couldn't help but appreciate Denny's success with the language but had to take a stand for his roomie's own good. "There isn't time for that. "You need to focus on getting hired by the Sheriff's Office, not on getting laid."

"The S.O. doesn't care about that shit," Denny insisted.

Luke could feel his anger rising but wasn't sure if it was aimed at Denny's puerile fixation on his penis or at himself for following Hartson's order to not tell his best friend about the sex crimes investigation. "You know as well as I do that what you did with your dick and with that stupid camera of yours are the main reasons you got in trouble with the PD."

"You told me that Browner and Biletnikoff had it in for me. I don't have that problem with the Sheriff," Denny said.

Luke's anger kept rising and clearly stemmed from the awkward position his knowledge of the special detail had placed him in. His decision not to tell Denny about it felt like a betrayal. But if he confided in his roommate and Biletnikoff or Browner found out about it somehow, he'd lose his job and Hartson, still on a probationary status as sergeant, would probably get demoted and sent to patrol Siberia somewhere. He wouldn't do anything to sabotage Hartson's career.

"You're too stupid for words sometimes," he said. "Jealousy is jealousy and people are bound to get pissed off because of your sex life no matter where you work."

"Lighten up, homey. You're just para-- What's that word?" Denny asked.

"Paranoid," Luke said and he could almost laugh at the irony. He knew for a fact that people were out to get Denny who was about to play into their hands by going to the beach in the middle of the night.

"Someone totally new every day?" he asked.

"No challenge otherwise," Denny said.

Luke sucked in a breath and let it out slowly as he counted to ten. "If that's your game, all I can do is stand along the sidelines and help you keep score," he said. "But, don't you care anything about love?"

"My mama loves me," Denny said. "Which covers the love part, everything else is about me gettin' some of that fine ass strange." He started toward the door. "I've been meaning to ask if you borrowed my flashlight."

"What would I want with your flashlight?" Luke asked.

"You didn't need it for work?"

"When did you see it last?"

"The last time I used it," Denny said.

Luke sighed. "When was that?"

Denny thought for a second. "I used it to spice up my under-the-covers fun a while ago." He grinned, gyrated his hips and shrugged. "But I don't remember when that was."

Luke shook his head slowly. "I haven't seen it. One of your lady friends probably helped herself as a memento of the best night of her life."

Those words occasioned a great big grin from Denny. "It'll turn up somewhere." He picked up his camera bag and turned the doorknob.

Luke checked the clock on the wall, opened his book and tried to read but started obsessing about an incident he'd witnessed when Denny was still on the department. The two of them had been staffing single officer units and had both ended up in the parking patio of the main police station at the same time. Denny had arrested a woman for driving under the influence of alcohol who had waist-length-hair the color of burgundy wine. Her flimsy tank top exposed smooth skin that could have easily been mistaken for a rich French Vanilla ice cream that Denny might have spooned over sliced peaches and eaten off her breasts.

She'd obviously sized Denny up correctly. As Luke passed by the car on his way to the report room he heard her cooing and seductive words. "If you don't put me in jail you can suck on my tits." It was an offer that many men would find hard to resist and Luke wondered if Denny could have turned it down if she'd made the offer on a dark street before their arrival at the station. Women, drunk and sober, in the disco or in the back of his police car, all threw themselves at Denny. Why in the world would he ever need to be a rapist?

# 43

T.D. HARTSON'S AFFAIR WITH BEVERLY SHIMMER had started inno-
cently enough as many serial trysts do. The Shimmers had quickly drifted
apart when J.R. couldn't comfort his wife over the drowning of their
three-year-old son in their backyard pool. Beverly blamed herself. So did
J.R., and the feckless comfort offered up by most family and friends was
comprised of ineffective assertions that the drowning was an accident
that could have happened to anybody. But it hadn't happened to anyone.
It had happened to Johnny when J.R. was at work and Beverly was in
charge and J.R. couldn't forgive his wife for letting it happen.

Hartson saw the outward evidence of the Shimmers' anguish and
did what he could to help but nothing existed that could stitch J.R.'s
broken jigsaw of a heart together again. When Hartson's efforts to talk
about Johnny fell flat, he'd nod and talk about a recent arrest, some tid-
bit that offered a little humor. When no laughter came, he tried talking
about the Turnbow shooting.

J.R.'s response would be to hoist another drink and complain about
Biletnikoff. When their shift activities allowed, Hartson would seek
J.R. out for meal breaks. He'd also urge him to meet at the One-Five-
Three Club after work and to invite Beverly along like in the old days.
Outwardly, Shimmer seemed OK some of the time in spite of the dark-
ening splotches under the eyes that suggested he was the bounty hunter
and sleep was a hiding fugitive.

Hartson often dropped by the Shimmers' three bedroom stucco home in their modest Clairemont neighborhood just to say hello. He'd be reassured when he entered the front door to see that the interior looked a lot tidier than the increasingly ragged lawn.

On one occasion, Shimmer lay huddled on the living room's harvest gold sofa, his socked foot bridging the gap between the cushions and an oak coffee table. Three ashtrays of Marlboro butts shared the table's surface with a half-empty Jack Daniels bottle and a drained tumbler. The only sound came from Shimmer's bourbon induced snoring.

Beverly walked into the room as he stood over his unconscious friend and he asked her how she was holding up. While Shimmer's mouth was a dam that kept his words and his grief blocked up, hers was a spigot that overflowed with anguish and remorse. She told him that Johnny had loved insects, and birds, and heavy equipment like earth movers and backhoes and cement mixers and dump trucks. Chocolate ice cream, especially the style that came in soft-swirled cones was his favorite. He hated spinach but had eaten the stuff that came in jars as an infant. Royal blue was his favorite color and she'd gone into the house for just a second to answer the phone and got too involved in the conversation.

"J.R. misses Johnny all day every day," she told him. "And he knows that I killed him through neglect, that I'm the one who didn't pay attention while our baby drowned."

When the two of them retreated to the kitchen for a cup of tea, they sat at a table next to a wall that was covered with a hand-painted, pale beach, breezy clouds and a little boy playing with a sand bucket. Beverly served a plate of Chips Ahoy cookies with the tea and kept on talking. "I guess you could say J.R. had a hand in Johnny's death." She stretched her lips into a tortured smile. "After all, he left him in the care of a careless mother."

She told Hartson that her husband had crawled into a sink-hole of grief and stayed there and wouldn't allow her in there with him. "There's no room inside him to share his grief and he wants no part of mine," she said. "He craves oblivion and I want it too, but not like him, alcohol won't do it for me. Besides, why do I deserve any consolation?" She picked up an unopened bottle of Jack Daniels from the table and twisted it in her hands. "I used to think we should have another baby. Oh, I knew it wouldn't be Johnny, but since we loved him so much we could love another one too, right? But J.R. won't touch me."

She reached for a cookie.

"When he's home and I'm in bed, I can hear the TV in the living room or him forcing ice cubes from the tray here in the kitchen. I used to get up and try spending a little time with him but he'd just sit there with a tumbler of bourbon in his left hand and the TV remote and a cigarette in his right. Sitting up with him was worse than trying to sleep alone."

"When he's here with me, I find myself wishing for the night to end. Then I start looking forward to his next graveyard shift so he'll be gone for the night."

Beverly looked Hartson in the eyes. "I don't know, maybe if he'd been able to save that woman things would be different. He still blames himself for that, you know."

Hartson fully understood the futility of failed attempts to save somebody. He nodded.

From that moment on, Hartson turned his efforts toward helping Beverly who clearly needed a shoulder to cry on. They'd meet twice a week for lunch at the Casa de Pico in Old Town where the Spaniards had long ago established a settlement. Tales of Johnny and the loss of him poured out of her over plates of chicken quesadillas, chile rellenos, rice, and refritos. The grief would roll over and through her again and she'd find a slightly different way to share her guilt.

Hartson knew these times were reserved for her, so he decided not to tell her about his son living with his ex-wife back in Chicago and how she'd waited until he'd been hired by the SDPD to tell him she was leaving him. He still drowned his sorrows in the bottle just like Shimmer did. But those stories were for another time and another place and he limited his alcohol intake to two beers when they were together.

"People have tried to help but they mostly want to talk, not listen and what they have to say comes up empty for me," Beverly said. "Our pastor's words were only a slight improvement on silence because he just kept telling us that Johnny's death was a part of God's plan. What sort of plan could God have that let me kill my baby?"

Hartson remembered from his Sunday school days that the impact of words was often as empty as the noises made by sounding brass and tinkling cymbals but he still had to try. He couldn't continue listening to her condemn herself without asking her to stop. "It really was an accident and you've got to forgive yourself." It was all he could think of to say but the sincerity of the effort tore through Beverly's defenses.

She started to cry and grasped and kissed his hand. "Thank you," she said. "I need real talk like that, not the phony stuff. And I've got to keep talking about Johnny if you're willing to listen. Otherwise it's like he never existed and that's a thought I can't bear to think. I can live with the guilt. It's the silence that nearly kills me sometimes." She picked up and turned the spoon she'd used to stir the lemon into her tea over and over again.

Up to that moment, Hartson had thought he could help J.R. by helping his wife. But now, seeing Beverly sitting across the table from him and looking so pitiful and alone, he wanted to reach out and hold her. Her eyes showed him that she felt the same way but he'd restrict their next contact to a movie as a protection from their shared vulnerabilities.

They met to see Smokey and the Bandit in the Loma Theater on Rosecrans Avenue. The reviews had said it was a silly comedy on wheels with an actor and actress who were fun to look at. It sounded like just the thing.

Hartson never went to a movie without loading up with popcorn and Milk Duds and that day was no exception. He added soft drinks to the gummy feast and they found a couple of seats in the middle of the house. The movie was just as advertised; mindless and fun and he thought it was a relief for Beverly's anguish but he stopped patting himself on the back when he saw her crying. When he put his arms around her, she reached up and kissed him like there was no one else in the crowded theater.

# 44

A CADRE OF PLAIN CLOTHES PATROL OFFICERS MET with sex crimes detectives in a utilitarian conference room on the second floor of San Diego's Community Concourse building. While the detail took on the appearance of having been convened by the lieutenant in charge of the Sex Crimes unit, the driving force was, in fact, Deputy Chief Browner who relished the idea of capturing Denny Durango, embarrassing Luke Jones and discrediting Chief Coleman. If Pantages' information turned out to help him identify and arrest Denny Durango as the rapist, it would seriously damage Chief Coleman's career and catapult Browner into a stronger position with Mayor Pete Pillson and City Councilman Dallas Cleveland.

Together with Councilman Cleveland, Pillson and his political operatives viewed construction of the convention center as a necessary stepping stone for Pillson's future bid for the U.S. Senate. Denny had recently embarrassed both men by arresting the mayor's top aide at a rally in Balboa Park designed to garner public support for the project. To add insult to the injury of all, Denny was still engaged in a part time, openly sexual relationship with the councilman's daughter.

If Denny were arrested, Browner's most important benefit would be the huge comeuppance for Chief Coleman who'd excoriated Browner over Denny's treatment during the investigation of the Balboa

Park incident. He'd also hurled not so veiled threats at Browner for manipulating Sergeant Biletnikoff into forcing Denny to resign.

Browner strode to the lectern and surveyed the room which had been specifically selected away from police headquarters to maintain the façade of a veil of secrecy about the operation. Several patrol supervisors had been charged with hand-selecting one or two of their officers, specifically for their abilities to keep their mouths shut about their clandestine activities.

From Northern Division, Sergeant Hartson had selected Hank Hunter who'd first tipped him off to the possibility that Denny was the suspect. Hartson had shared that information with a Sex Crimes supervisor and the special detail was the result.

From Central Division, Sergeant Biletnikoff had selected Officers Andee Bradford and Dick Arenas, allegedly for their circumspection and investigative skills. In reality, Biletnikoff had selected Bradford to temporarily rid himself of her constant complaining about sexual harassment by the male officers on the squad. He'd chosen Arenas to reward him for his loyalty, see if there was a way to implicate Luke Jones in the rape fiasco, and keep tabs on Bradford. It mattered to Biletnikoff not at all that Arenas was the main object of Bradford's harassment complaints.

The investigation carried a heightened sense of urgency since word was out among the department's supervisors that the beach rapist was most likely either a current or a former cop. Orders to keep that information secret notwithstanding, Browner knew that rumors would soon start flying among members of the press and the P.D. rank and file. Once the media started openly kicking the theory around, any additional cases in the rape series would stain the wholesale reputation of San Diego County law enforcement. At least Dr. Pantages' information narrowed the potential suspect pool considerably, allowing officers to focus their efforts.

"You people have been hand-selected for an extremely important mission," Browner told them. "You all should have a package with details of the beach rape series in front of you. Now, what you don't know is that Dr. Pantages has put a lot of work into developing a profile of the suspect. You'll find those details in your packets with one exception. We've deliberately left out one extremely important aspect of the profile. Dr. Pantages is convinced that our suspect is either former or current law enforcement. We don't know much about him other than he always wears a mask, is extremely fit and athletic, always seems to know whenever any law enforcement is active along the beaches and utilizes police tactics.

For reasons we won't go into right now, we believe that the suspect may be Denny Durango. In case you don't remember him, he's the one who arrested the mayor's chief aide a while ago. What he did was a huge embarrassment to our department and, I shouldn't be saying this, but Durango's roommate is a young officer who's working Central Division right now. We can't say so for sure, but if Durango is our rapist, there's a good chance his roommate is helping Durango cover up the crimes.

"Some of you will be conducting surveillance along the beaches and some of you will be following Durango. While we won't be actively following his roommate, it's extremely important that you let us know if you see anyone else who might be involved in the rapes.

Sergeant Duran will be handing out your specific assignments once you've broken up into your respective groups. I can't stress enough that this operation has to be held in the strictest confidence and that the department wants to get out ahead of the press by announcing a successful arrest."

# 45

ANDEE BRADFORD PARKED A WHITE DETECTIVE'S SEDAN behind Luke
Jones as he sat at Horton Plaza filling out his daily journal.

"Andee, it's great to see you," Luke said as she approached his open
window. "What's up?"

"I'm working a special detail," Andee said. "It involves Denny Durango which is why I wanted to talk to you. We're under orders not to
tell anyone about it so I could get in serious trouble if word gets out
about what I'm saying."

Luke liked and respected Andee for her inner strength and ability
to stand up for her rights and would never place her in a vulnerable
position. She was about as tall as a walking stick and her breasts commanded men to look at them instead of into her eyes and, for no other
reason than her appearance, surviving her chosen career was a difficult
task. But she'd met all of her challenges so far and Luke didn't expect
that to change.

"Why don't you sit down and tell me what's on your mind." Luke
said.

She shook her head. "I'm here because I feel like I owe it to you to
tell you what's going on but sitting in your car's not a good idea right
now."

Puzzled, Luke kept his mouth shut.

"I think what's happening is wrong," Andee said. "But orders are orders and I don't have any choice about this special sex crimes detail they have me working."

Luke nodded.

"You know about it?" Andee asked.

"I've got some friends who keep me in the loop," Luke said.

"Somehow, somebody got it into their head that Denny's the likely suspect, and Browner said some things at lineup designed to implicate you if Denny gets arrested."

The depths that Biletnikoff and Browner were willing to stoop to suddenly seemed unbelievable. "They're trying to kill two toads with one skipping stone," Luke said.

"These guys are lower than dirt," Andee said as she swallowed. "Part of the detail will be on stake out along the beaches and the rest of us are going to keep an eye on Denny twenty-four hours a day." She bit her lower lip. "It's just wrong. You know Denny's not my idea of prince charming but I know he's not a rapist and I've been assigned to the team that's keeping an eyeball on him."

"This is starting to get scary," Luke said.

Andee pressed her lips tight and nodded.

# 46

LUKE CLOSED THE DOOR TO HARTSON'S OFFICE at Northern Division.

"I've only got a minute," Hartson said. "What's up?"

"Denny is what's up. I know about the special detail surveilling him and that Browner's said some things at their first lineup trying to set me up to take a fall as well."

Luke saw a flicker of anger evident in Hartson's eyes and suspected that he wanted to kick Browner's ass for trashing Luke.

"This is really starting to get ugly," Luke said.

"It's way beyond my control now," Hartson said. "It's looking like Browner and Coleman are going at each other and you and Denny are their pawns. Browner asked some of the commands to hand-pick officers for the assignment. We're short on people so I only sent Hunter. Guess who selected the people from Central."

"Biletnikoff." Luke could practically feel his body sinking through the floor as he said it.

"You got it in one guess and you know he's at least as anxious to screw you as Browner is," Hartson said.

"There must be a way to stop this," Luke said.

"Nobody trusts your judgment the way I do, Luke, and if you tell me Denny's not the rapist, I believe you. But there isn't anything I can do to help you out on this except to tell you to stay away from it. It's way above my pay grade."

"I've got to do something to help Denny," Luke said.

"You need to focus on protecting yourself," Hartson said. "Even if you could help Denny, you'd be accused of bias and potentially criminally bad judgment if Denny does get arrested."

"I'm only biased because I know the guy well enough to swear he's not a rapist," Luke insisted.

"For Denny's sake and for your own good, you need to stay out of it. You're not even supposed to know that Denny's a suspect. I told you that in confidence."

"I haven't told anyone and you still haven't told me who pointed to him as the rapist."

"And I'm not going to because it's not something you need to know."

"Maybe that person has an axe to grind," Luke said. "Have you considered that?"

"Don't be ridiculous. The officer doesn't have anything against Denny. In fact, I'd say it's just the opposite."

"Then there's no reason you shouldn't tell me," Luke insisted.

"That's not going to happen."

"You know I won't give up until I find out who it is," Luke said.

Hartson did know and, for the first time in their friendship, Luke's stubbornness really pissed him off. "This could end your career and you need to stay away from it, Luke." Hartson started to walk away but turned after a couple steps. "Is there anything you need to tell me?" he demanded.

"No." Luke winced at Hartson's directness.

"Really? Denny went to the beach last night. Were you going to tell me that?"

"He had a date," Luke said, "and you were following him already? When were you going to tell me about that?"

Hartson swallowed.

"Was there a rape that night?" Luke demanded.

"You know there wasn't," Hartson said.

Luke concentrated on openly displaying his disgust as he shook his head. "I'm out of here. I'll tell you that much," he said as his parting shot.

He saw Hunter coming out of the locker room and waved him over as he was leaving.

"How's it going? Are you riding with the Sarge again?" Hunter asked.

"I hear you're on the sex crimes detail," Luke said. It wasn't a question. It was an accusation.

Hunter nodded.

"You weren't going to tell me about following Denny?" Luke tried keeping the building bitterness out of his voice.

"I follow orders. You know that, Luke. Don't let this thing eat at you. I doubt Denny's good for it," Hunter said.

"Do you know who dropped Denny's name at lineup the other night?" Luke asked.

"I was off then," Hunter responded.

Hadn't Hartson said that Hunter was at lineup that night? Luke could feel the tension rising in his muscles. He reached up to massage the recurring tension headache at the base of his skull he'd initially experienced at the scene of his first suicide. Something was decidedly wrong. He just didn't know what. "Whoever the guy is, he's got the special detail twisted into knots, I can tell you that much," Luke said. "I'm told the theory is that the rapist is working his way south down the coast and is likely to hit again on Thursday. I've looked at the data the Crime Analysis unit puts out and that conclusion supports the data," Luke said. "But he hasn't hit for a couple weeks now which tells me he's reassessing his patterns to account for law enforcement's stepped up response. I believe he'll avoid heading south and hit on different days than he's hit so far."

Hunter half smirked. "You always were a little smarter than everybody else in the room," he said. "I'll suggest that we concentrate our efforts a little further north if I can get them to listen."

"That's a good idea," Luke said. "While you're at it, you might also suggest concentrating on days other than Thursdays. It's time to start thinking like the rapist instead of like bureaucrats."

# 47

LUKE REMEMBERED A BIT OF HIS SAN DIEGO HISTORY as he entered the doors to the Pickwick Hotel. Charles Wesley Grise had established the Limited San Diego and Imperial Valley Stage line in 1911, which used a touring car to transport passengers from the coast to the desert farming valley a little more than one-hundred miles away. As the company grew into a major stage line by 1915, the name changed to the Pickwick Stages, complete with a series of hotels they constructed along their stage routes. The first one was located at Union Square in San Francisco and later put to use by Dashiell Hammett in *The Maltese Falcon.*

A year after erection of the San Francisco hotel, Pickwick Stages opened a two-towered gothic hotel at the corner of First Avenue and Broadway in downtown San Diego. By 1928, Pickwick Stages had constructed two radio towers on the roof of the building and broadened its business base from automobile terminals and hotels to radio broadcasting. Art Linkletter, who later starred in "Kids Say the Darndest Things" began his television career from the KGB studios on the Pickwick Hotel's first and second floors.

Things had certainly deteriorated at the Pickwick by the time Luke got the radio call about an abandoned skeleton in one of the guest rooms. The aging front office manager approached with his hand extended, looking like someone who'd once taken care of himself until he got frazzled down by the wear and tear of a difficult life. He wore a three piece, chalk stripe navy suit that frayed slightly at the lapels and a multi-colored, diagonally striped tie that was held tight against his wrinkled shirt by a stage-coach shaped tie pin. He'd skillfully folded a red pocket square into three-points and tucked it meticulously into his jacket pocket.

"How do you do?" he said. "I'm Augustus Quarles. It's terrible what I found, just terrible. I've worked here for twenty years and thought I'd seen everything. You know how it is people come to a hotel and feel they can misbehave without consequence."

"I know how it is," Luke agreed.

"You name it. Music, loud parties, women coming and going in various degrees of dishabille," Quarles said.

Luke couldn't help but laugh a little. "Yes," he said. "People should definitely keep their clothes on in the public areas."

Quarles smiled broadly. "Oh, and they complain about everything like lords and ladies of the manor. The bed's too soft, the bed's too hard. The lighting is too dim, the lighting is too bright. How come you don't have cheeseburgers on the room service menu? The ice isn't cold enough. It's always…"

Luke put up his hand to call a truce.

"But in all these years, I've never found anything to beat this," Quarles said it at the same time the chatter from an approaching handi-talkie could be heard. Luke looked up to see Bob Fiedler coming his way.

Mr. Quarles led the officers to the elevators keeping up his chatter as they ascended and trudged down a long, carpeted hallway a few floors up, leaving Luke to wonder if Quarles talked incessantly all the time or if his oral outpouring was a result of the stressful situation.

"More than one guest has claimed ghost sightings over the years. There's been a lot of nonsense about a ghostly white flapper drifting along the corridors, but those glimpses have only happened on the fourth floor, which does make you wonder, I guess. Here we are." Quarles stopped in front of a door marked 509 and turned the key.

Fiedler took the key from Quarles' hand. "We'll need you to remain outside the room for now sir," he said. "But we'd appreciate it if you'd stay close in case we need you."

"That's OK with me," Quarles said. "One look at that was enough for me."

There was no mistaking the headless skeleton that was laid out on the bed. The room also contained a mahogany dresser and night stands, and a writing table that completed the bedroom suite sat near the window facing Broadway.

The Pickwick Hotel in general, and Room 509 in particular, had both seen better days but last night's guests had turned the room into a disaster. The bedspread still covered the bed, but it dripped all over with dried, red candle wax.

The wax drippings overlaid empty wine bottles and crushed cans of Old Milwaukee beer. There were several boxes of half eaten pizzas in various parts of the room but the neatly folded skeleton undoubtedly commanded center attention. It rested on the bed in an almost reverential pose. Its shredded funeral attire held the bones together and the bones emanated a musty smell and showcased the macabre candle drippings that hung from the ribs like stalactites in an underground cavern. But it was the missing part that stood out. Where was the head?

Fiedler stepped into the hallway to speak with Quarles. "The good news is that apparently no one was killed here. But we haven't found the head. Have you seen it?"

"No," Quarles said. "I closed the door as soon as I saw what was on the bed and called you."

"How many people were registered in the room," Fiedler asked.

"Just the one."

"Was it a man or a woman?"

"The person who registered was a young man of about twenty,"

Quarles answered. "Judging from his haircut, I'd imagine he was either a sailor or a marine."

"We'll need his name," Fiedler said.

"I've taken the liberty of getting that for you," Quarles said. He handed Fiedler a registration card with the name of Perry White printed on it in blue ink.

"Great Caesar's ghost," Fiedler said.

"I beg your pardon?"

"Nothing," Fiedler answered. "Did you meet Mr. White?"

"Briefly," Quarles said indignantly. "Messing with bodies for goodness sakes, do you think you'll be able to track him down?"

"I doubt it," Fiedler said.

"And why is that?"

"Because Perry White's a comic book character," Fiedler answered before he walked back into the room.

"I think we've solved the mystery of where the body came from," Luke told him. "Dispatch says that someone dug up a grave out at Mount Hope Cemetery and snatched a body yesterday. I've found a couple crucifixes, some skull and crossbones and a few other weird things with occult connections. I'm betting there was some kind of séance here last night."

"There's nothing better than a séance with pizza and cheap beer," Fiedler said. "Did you find the skull anywhere?"

"It's not here," Luke said.

"Did you look under the bed?"

"Under the bed?" Luke asked incredulously.

"Yes, under the bed," Fiedler insisted.

"I didn't think of it," Luke said.

"That's because you're the naïve rookie and I'm the savvy senior guy," Fiedler said with a laugh.

Luke dropped to his hands and knees to survey the space between the floor and the bed. "It's too dark. I can't see anything," he said.

Fiedler handed Luke the small flashlight he carried on his gun belt.

Luke flicked it on and tried again. "It's under here all right," he said and kept the light beam trained on the empty spaces where the eyes used to be. "Do you think it's OK if I crawl in and get it, or should we wait for the coroner?"

Fiedler chuckled. "This guy's been dead a long time. We'll be dealing with the cemetery not with the coroner."

Luke crawled a little further under the bed, snatched the skull and pulled it out holding it in the palm of his hand. He pushed himself to his knees and decided it was time for a little performance as he contemplated the skull. "Alas, poor Yorick! I knew him, Horatio: a fellow of infinite jest, of most excellent fancy…"

"Enough," Fiedler said. "No wonder some of the guys think you're a weirdo." He reached for the skull. "I don't suppose Mr. Shakespeare would have anything to say about what a nut job you are."

"I don't know what he'd say about me but I know what he'd say about you under the circumstances." Luke picked up a candle stub and held it close to his face. "You are as a candle, the better part burnt out," he said as the van crew from the graveyard arrived.

# 48

THE REPORT ROOM POPPED WITH ACTIVITY, which was an absolute pain in Biletnikoff's ass. He had more important things demanding his attention than the reams of penny ante paperwork being tossed at him for his approval, like that stupid Luke Jones. What he wouldn't give to rid himself of that floating turd in a river. Who'd that loudmouth rookie think he was? Going over his head, and questioning his authority all the time. No rookie should get away with the things he did.

He'd figure out a way to show that punk a thing or two one of these days. There had to be a way to put him his place. He was too arrogant to ever turn into a bona fide officer. That stupid Lt. Rood didn't know anything about discipline and wouldn't let Biletnikoff do his job by meting out a little administrative justice. She'd never been worth spit as a police officer and now she was an affirmative action lieutenant. Women shouldn't be anything but rape decoys and meter maids.

Look what had happened when police departments let women think of themselves like real police officers. They stole a good man's lieutenant position and protected punk ass rookies who should be bounced out of the department and into the street.

Finding his coffee cold, he crossed over to the ever-simmering pot of black sludge. He had to do something. He couldn't turn off his anger.

Where did Jones get off? That stunt he'd pulled with Arenas over the arrest report was over the top. That rookie punk probably thought no one would report him for the insubordination but Arenas had told him. And the whole incident occurred because Jones came to the job with some sort of fancy college degree. No one could tell him anything. And that Shakespeare nonsense! What good had knowing about Shakespeare ever done anyone? All it did for Luke Jones was fill his mouth with sixteen dollar words that he liked to show off.

The world would never be right until Jones joined his sex-crazed pal Denny Durango in some civilian line of work. Biletnikoff was sure it had been Jones who'd stolen those photos of Tina Cleveland out of his desk. Going into his office and into his desk and threatening him with that note – the guy was no better than a two-bit burglar. His gut burned and not just from the crummy brew.

Stealing the pictures and threatening to expose the urinating incident in the Lieutenant's office showed that Jones had no redeeming qualities and wasn't fit to wear the uniform. That punk always had some sort of hobgoblin looking out for him. First it was Hartson then it was Shimmer. Now it was that dike Rood who he knew was queer because she'd always turned him down. It was the only reasonable explanation.

# 49

LIEUTENANT ROOD HAD KICKED LUKE'S QUARTERLY evaluation back and demanded that Biletnikoff raise the overall mark from "Improvement Needed" to "Superior" and Biletnikoff didn't want it getting back to Jones how pissed he was. He'd have to wait to get even. That arrogant loudmouth even screwed with his getting-pissed-off schedule. A little while ago he'd thought that pairing Jones off with Shimmer would make him crazy. Instead, Shimmer had sucked up to the younger, more dominant Jones and the two of them turned into the best of buddies.

Too many people around the department treated Jones like a hero for shooting that crazy drunk a while ago and allegedly saving Shimmer's life. It was probably a bad shooting but there was no way to prove it with Shimmer standing up for Jones. Shimmer was an easy target for manipulation and Jones probably reminded him at every turn that he'd saved his life.

Shimmer had traipsed a long way toward hell since his little boy died. And now his wife was running around with Hartson but Shimmer's head was too messed up to see it. The little boy's death had ruined the marriage, even if Shimmer didn't know it yet.

Someone needed to tell Shimmer about his wife and Hartson. Biletnikoff would have already told the poor guy himself, except he didn't want to add to the little man's troubles. But there came a time when holding back bad news was crueler than telling the unsavory truth.

Luke Jones had to know about the affair but had obviously kept the information secret. What kind of friendship was that? Biletnikoff had thought it was great at the sex crimes briefing when Chief Browner listed Durango as a possible serial rapist and revealed that a current officer might be concealing his guilt. Everyone there had to know he was talking about Luke Jones. He shoved the paperwork across the table and sat up tall. How else could Denny dodge all the extra patrols and decoys without Jones feeding him inside information? It only made sense that if Durango was the rapist Jones had to be helping him.

Suddenly getting rid of Jones was no longer about purging the department of another worthless rookie. He had to be exposed for his part in a hideous criminal conspiracy.

Biletnikoff saw his duty clearly now. He needed to get the proof to put Denny in jail and, at the very least, get Jones fired. He crossed the squad room in a few strides when Shimmer walked in, his hand still in a cast, and told him he needed to see him in the sergeant's office.

"I need you to do something for Chief Browner and for the good of the department," he announced after he'd shut the door.

"What's up Sarge?" Shimmer asked.

Biletnikoff felt a twinge of guilt for a second. No. The sooner Shimmer figured out who his real friends were the better.

"You remember Denny Durango?" Biletnikoff asked.

"I remember Luke's roommate, what about him?"

"You remember that he resigned from the department?"

"I remember that he's Luke's friend and I was probably too strict on his evaluations."

"They're not just roommates. Luke's his friend," Biletnikoff said. "I suppose you think Luke's your friend too."

"Luke's a great guy."

"Not as great as you think he is," Biletnikoff insisted.

"Luke's been nothing but a good friend to me since we got our troubles straightened out."

"Do good friends lie to you?" Biletnikoff asked.

"Luke's never lied to me about anything."

"We'll get back to that in a minute. "You know about the beach rape series, right?"

"What's that got to do with Luke or Denny?"

"Have you heard the latest on the rapist? It's supposed to be a secret but I'm sure word's getting out," Biletnikoff answered.

"I know he only attacks couples and makes the girls tie their dates up before the rapes."

"What you don't know is that Dr. Pantages did a profile on the suspect and thinks he's either a current or a former cop."

Shimmer raised his eyebrows. "She said that?"

"And Durango fits the guy's description. There's some other stuff we know that ties Durango to the series but I can't tell you about that right now. I know you don't want to believe any of this and I don't blame you. I didn't want to believe it either but it fits doesn't it? Think about it, defiling those women like that. You remember those naked photos of the councilman's daughter that Durango took?"

Shimmer ran his tongue across his lips, swallowed and nodded.

"What kind of a guy would do a thing like that?" Biletnikoff asked. "You know as well as me that he's the same type who'd humiliate women in front of their boyfriends to show he's superior to everyone else."

Shimmer's eyes widened.

"It all fits," Biletnikoff said. "And there's something you can do to help out."

"I don't know what to think about all this," Shimmer said.

"You don't have to think," Biletnikoff said. "I'll tell you how you can help. Durango will be getting hired by the Sheriff's Office pretty soon if we don't do the right thing and stop it. Imagine how much more dangerous he'd be if he does get hired. He'd have a gun and a badge and be privy to all the details of the rape investigation. It's bad enough that he's a former cop, but how much worse would it be if he goes active duty again?"

"I'm not saying I'm buying what you're saying, but what has Luke got to do with any of this?"

Biletnikoff calculated his answer. "It may be a stretch to say that Luke's actively helping Denny get away with what he's doing. Maybe Durango's just using him in some way that Luke doesn't know about, like pumping him for information that keeps him from getting caught."

"Luke's too smart for that," Shimmer said.

"J.R., you know I'm your friend, don't you?"

"Sure, Sarge."

"What I'm about to say is for your own good," Biletnikoff said.

"Go ahead." Shimmer's voice was barely audible.

"I hate to be the one to tell you this, but since everybody knows but you..."

"Knows what?" Shimmer asked.

"About your wife. There, I've said it and I'm sorry but it had to be done," Biletnikoff said.

"Knows what about my wife? What are you talking about?" Shimmer's face showed physical pain as if someone had pounded a hammer against his broken hand.

"Knows that she's running around with Hartson and Luke has been helping them keep it from you. You should hear them laugh and joke behind your back."

All Biletnikoff actually did was plant a seed of doubt but Shimmer's face instantaneously registered his belief that Luke Jones was a traitor. Now it would be easy to set Shimmer up to go after a little revenge.

"But at least we can--you can--keep Durango from becoming a sheriff's deputy and protect the women of this county while you're at it," Biletnikoff said.

Shimmer's response came in a hoarse whisper. "What can I do?"

"Luke broke into my desk and took the photos of Councilman Cleveland's daughter. I need you to get them back so I can use them to keep Durango from getting hired by the Sheriff's Office."

"The photos?" Shimmer looked pitifully at his sergeant. "I can get the photos back I guess."

Biletnikoff knew his mission was almost accomplished. "Bring them to me when you get them. But you can't let any of what we've said slip out to Jones or everything we're trying to do will be messed up."

# 50

Luke found Hartson in a booth at the Spot, an eclectic eatery in La Jolla located at the southeast corner of Prospect Street and Girard Avenue. Luke had befriended the chef during his trainee days and the joint served his favorite thin crust pizza with a topping of extra spicy pepperoni and green olives. The mini-skirted waitress with the Goldie Hawn hairdo and extra tight T-shirt added a lot to the ambience. He settled back into the booth with a glass of merlot in hand hoping that Hartson would find a way to kick start the conversation.

The restaurant had a full bar, a few tables in the center floor near the gas fireplace and several comfortable leather booths. The lighting was subdued and the televisions were constantly tuned to various sporting events. The menu consisted of several pages with a seemingly infinite variety of foods to choose from.

The two men sat in a booth at the back of the restaurant near the public restrooms. Luke normally commandeered the seat with the most complete view of the interior of the restaurant but gave that privilege to the senior officer. In his short time as a cop he'd learned not to expose his back to the front door or to other patrons without another cop to keep an eye on things for him.

The waitress tapped her pen against the order pad and Luke ordered his pizza without benefit of the menu. Hartson agreed to share the pizza and ordered a dinner salad and gin martini with extra olives to round out his dinner.

Luke sat silently while Hartson ate the salad like a starving man and could tell that his former training officer was as uncomfortable as he was. Luke had dropped a hint of what he wanted to talk about when he'd called Hartson to arrange the meeting and the tension was building slowly.

Hartson finally established eye contact as he pushed his empty salad plate to the center of the table. "Look, Luke, I'm sorry, but I can't pull off your transfer to Northern this shift change, I've been told to expect someone else."

"That's interesting I guess," Luke said. "But you know that's not what I wanted to talk about."

The waitress interrupted by setting the pizza down between them.

"I need to talk to you about Shimmer's wife."

Hartson held his martini glass between them like a shield.

"I think Shimmer may be the only one on the department who doesn't know you're sleeping with her. Is that any way to treat a friend?" Luke demanded.

"How did you know?" Hartson asked.

"You dropped a hint a few months ago," Luke said. Then he decided to stop being obtuse. "Devree tells me that Biletnikoff's told Shimmer about it and blamed me for keeping it from him."

Hartson nodded. "It's got to be him or one of his bunch," Hartson said. "Listen, Luke. We didn't plan it – it just happened."

"I'm sure it'll make Shimmer feel better knowing that his friend's sleeping with his wife was an accident."

"Honest, Luke, it just happened. I don't know any other way to explain it. I tried being there for both of them after their baby drowned, but J.R. wouldn't talk to me and Beverly needed to talk. I just listened with no idea that we'd fall in love."

"You should have stopped seeing her the second you knew you were developing feelings for her," Luke said.

"It's not that simple. I needed to be with her like her husband couldn't be. And I didn't know she had romantic feelings for me until she kissed me in a crowded movie theater. I never would have told her how I felt, but it was too late by then."

"I don't care how it happened," Luke said. "You two betrayed Shimmer and you should have at least gone to him and told him. He should never have had to hear this from someone else."

"We'd planned on telling him this week because we're moving in together."

Luke wanted to reach across the table and smack Hartson in the face. Instead he infused vitriol into his words. "How long have you two been planning to do this?"

"A while now," Hartson said.

"Are you aware that the entire department knew before Shimmer and me and he thinks that I've betrayed him?"

"I wanted to tell him from the start but Beverly kept saying the timing wasn't right."

"I can't believe I'm hearing this from you," Luke said. Hartson had turned out to be another solid stone idol with feet of clay and sticks. Was everyone like this? He thought about the youth pastor in his father's church when he was ten who'd been honored as "Man of the Year" by the ecumenical council. Later that month, the Man of the Year ran off to Mexico with another man's wife as his own wife lay in the hospital giving birth to a baby girl. The big surprise wasn't that the pastor's betrayal hadn't killed his wife. Nor that the congregation forgave him and took him back after his paramour toddled back to her husband. No, the big surprise was that the pastor's wife took him back.

Now Shimmer was suffering from the loss of his son and Hartson was managing to act as selfishly as the erstwhile Man of the Year. Could it be that people weren't capable of being loyal? All Luke could do was to try and hold himself to a high standard of authenticity.

He finished his second glass of wine and pushed his plate away, took some bills from his wallet and laid them on the table. Then he stood up, "I'd hoped for better from you. That's all I can say."

# 51

"So it appears you've weaseled out again." Sergeant Biletnikoff scooted his chair under the desk after he stood and leaned close to Luke who reciprocated until Biletnikoff backed off. "Lt. Rood took it on herself to go back and review your previous reviews and made me change your rating." If Biletnikoff expected a response, he was disappointed.

"Dick Arenas told me how you ran to her to get a report signed that he felt needed improvement," Biletnikoff continued.

Once again, Biletnikoff received silence as Luke's response.

"I guess I should have expected this." Biletnikoff tossed the revised evaluation on the desk in front of Luke for his signature. "You're nothing but a weasel."

Luke decided it was time to end his silence embargo. "What has Lt. Rood's scrutiny of your evaluation got to do with me?" Luke asked. "You're just pissed because you don't like me. It's as simple as that."

"You bet I'm pissed. You've got no business being on the police force. You don't have any respect for your superiors and you display extremely poor judgment," Biletnikoff said.

"Odd that the lieutenant disagrees with you," Luke said. "It's not my fault that she reversed your rating." Luke glanced to make sure that no one was in ear shot. "You just can't stand the fact that she called you out as a petty tyrant."

Biletnikoff's sneer turned into a gruesome smile. "Well it's too damn bad that I'm fixing you good just like I did before Jones."

"You can't get the evaluation reversed, give it up," Luke said.

"Pay attention smart guy, I said I'd fix you like I did before."

It took a second for Luke to process what Biletnikoff had said. "You can't mess with Denny? He's not under your thumb anymore," Luke said, but the worry must have registered on his face. Was Biletnikoff planning on getting Denny into trouble over the rapes or did he know that Denny was about to get hired by the Sheriff's Office?

Biletnikoff grinned. "I guess you weren't aware that new little pal of yours got into your equipment bag and gave the Tina Cleveland photos back to me. I'm not sure how, but somehow the Sheriff's Office got a hold of them after that."

"What're you talking about? Shimmer doesn't have the photos, you do."

"Cut the bullshit, rookie. You and I both know you stole those photos out of my desk a while ago and Shimmer just took them back."

"I don't know what you're talking about," Luke said.

"I know you're lying because your lips are moving," Biletnikoff said. "Now, get out of my office.

# 52

THINKING THAT THE LOCAL COP UNIVERSE NEEDED his special brand of intervention to set things on course, Paul Devree, the actual thief of the photos, skipped his after-hours workout to focus on a higher calling. His search for Shimmer ended at his first stop, the One-Five-Three Club.

Shimmer shifted his attention from his boilermaker to Devree as he approached the bar. The little guy actually looked worse than usual. The blackened circles under his eyes had grown deeper and darker and a noticeable patch of dry skin caressed his cheek and stretched along part of his neck.

"Good to see you," Shimmer said as he swallowed a shot of bourbon before setting the empty glass onto the bar.

"You won't think so in a minute," Devree answered as he sat on the stool next to the older man.

Shimmer's voice was unusually high and his words teetered on the verge of a stammer. "Hey look, I, I know you gave me those naked photos of Tina Cleveland so I could give them to Luke, which I did. I just took them back, that's all."

Devree ordered a beer. "Why is that?"

Shimmer's head retracted part way into his neck, making him resemble a turtle disappearing into itself. "I had to do what I did, but how did you know that I did it?" Shimmer mumbled.

"I make a point of knowing what goes on around here," Devree said. "Why did you screw the guy who saved your life and turned into a good friend?"

"He's not my friend."

"He tells me he's your friend and he acts like a friend. Is there a better definition than that?" Devree asked.

"You'd understand if you knew what I know," Shimmer said.

"Did you give those photos back to Biletnikoff to bitch Luke or to screw Denny out of his chance to get hired by the Sheriff's Office? Because you managed to do both at the same time."

"Biletnikoff told me I'd be doing a personal favor for Chief Browner and protecting a lot of women at the same time," Shimmer said. "Besides, Luke hid Beverly's affair with Hartson from me."

Devree pushed himself up from the chair. "I'm going to take a piss and when I get back you'd better start making sense." With no bartender in sight, he walked behind the bar and grabbed a couple Coronas and swallowed about half of his as he set the other one in front of Shimmer before heading towards the restroom.

"You're an idiot if you believe that about Luke," Devree said when he returned.

"I have it on good authority," Shimmer said.

Devree raised his eyebrow, an internal sign that he was trying to contain his anger. "Does that authority happen to be Constantin Biletnikoff?"

"Yes," Shimmer said, "but--"

"But nothing," Devree shot back. "Next thing I know you'll believe that crap being spread around that Denny's the rape suspect."

Shimmer's eyes blinked like an old fashioned cash machine registering a transaction.

"Did Biletnikoff tell you that too?" Devree asked.

"It's more than that," Shimmer said, but as he said it the conviction of his manufactured belief disappeared from his countenance.

This amounted to about all the horse crap Devree could take at the moment. "If this is about Hartson and Beverly, Luke had nothing to do with that?"

"How do you know?"

Devree could almost reach out and caress the pain that surrounded Shimmer like an inflated bubble. "I think everyone on the department knew about it except for you and Luke." Devree decided it would take a lot more beer to get through this mess, went behind the bar, poured a pitcher and grabbed a couple glasses.

"What do you mean Luke didn't know about it? Biletnikoff told me he was their go-between."

Devree slammed his empty beer bottle onto the bar. "You're too stupid for words sometimes." he said. "Luke didn't know anything about it until word started getting out that Biletnikoff was turning you into his butt-boy. When he found out why, he confronted Hartson and called him a traitor."

Shimmer's features looked like they were sliding off his face. If he'd heard this from just about anyone but Devree he'd never have believed it, but Devree was always a straight shooter. "Biletnikoff told me that Denny's the rapist and Luke could be helping him get away with it."

Devree wanted to slap some sense into Shimmer but his friend's eyes displayed a chasm of emptiness where a smile used to rest. Where Shimmer saw only confusion, Devree found clarity. "They think Denny's the rapist and Luke's helping him? Of all the stupid things I've heard in my life, there's nothing dumber than that. And you bought that bucket of Shinola about Luke?"

"People tell me he's been poking fun at me behind my back," Shimmer said.

"And who's been telling you that, you stupid peckerwood?" Devree asked as he strode off toward the men's room.

# 53

LUKE STOOD ON THE FRONT STOOP OF A PALE YELLOW house in the stylish neighborhood of Kensington. Sibyl shared the place with her best friend and he'd just decided he was colossally stupid for arriving at her place unannounced. He was about to leave when the front door opened unexpectedly.

"Can I help you?" The question came from a svelte woman who looked as if she'd modeled her hairstyle and color after the Olympic skating champion Dorothy Hamill.

"Is Sibyl here?"

Before the Dorothy Hamill doppelganger could answer, Luke heard Sibyl's voice coming from the interior of the house. "Luke! This is a surprise!"

"So, you're Luke," the woman holding the door said as she sized him up from head to toe. "This isn't really a good time but I guess you'd better come in any way." She stepped aside and led Luke into the dining room.

Sibyl stood between two neatly dressed men who appeared to be in their mid-twenties. She wore a denim skirt and a white peasant blouse that was shot through with vibrant red strands of chiles. Her sandal laces wound up her legs to her knees and she wore silver and turquoise earrings and bracelets that matched her squash blossom necklace.

"I can see my timing's bad," Luke said. "I'll call later in the week."

"Nonsense," Sibyl shot back. "We're just sitting down to dinner and we've got plenty." Her bracelets tinkled as she gestured nervously towards a chair at the table.

"I should have called." Luke suddenly felt queasy. He'd come without calling, interrupted a double date and started feeling like one of those hapless circus clowns who trips over his own feet and explodes his balloons at inopportune times. The doubts he'd silenced on the drive over suddenly started screaming for his attention. If only Sibyl's housemate hadn't preemptively opened the door. Sure, he'd stood at the threshold like a dummy but that didn't mean she needed to open the door when he hadn't even knocked.

He calmed himself by taking in the room. The dark and polished wood floors contrasted with the ivory walls and wainscoting and projected an elegant air. He wondered if Sibyl or her roommate had chosen the colors and which one had selected the old-fashioned Victorian furnishings. The classy home was occupied by two stylish women and provided a stark contrast to the almost unsavory bachelor pad he shared with Denny.

While Luke tried to think of something to say, he remembered that Sibyl had said she rented a room in the home she shared with her best friend Daphne and Daphne's boyfriend Rex. Daphne worked as a flight attendant and Rex attended law school.

Luke walked toward the two men and extended his hand. "I'm Luke Jones and I'm intruding," he said. "I just wanted to say a quick hello to Sibyl. I can do that another time."

"Please stay," Sibyl told him. "Daphne, you remember that I mentioned Luke?" Daphne's chuckle indicated that Sibyl was the mistress of understatement. "I remember," she said.

"Please ask him to stay," Sibyl said.

Daphne wisped a strand of hair from her forehead. She cut an attractive figure and was essentially the same height as Sibyl but her skin lacked the evanescent glow of her more glamorous roommate. Where

Sibyl's face and neck consisted of softly rounded curves, hers shot out at slight angles. Although her pale rose t-shirt over light blue jeans didn't add vibrancy to her persona, Luke decided she was probably strikingly attractive when she was out of Sybil's orbit.

Daphne smiled. "Yes, please stay, Luke. Right, Rex, we do want him to stay don't we?"

"Yes, of course we do," Rex said. The sincerity of his invitation was as thin as his handshake. His facial features were aquiline and refined and he'd retained his teenage wispiness the way some men manage to do years after reaching manhood. His jeans and polo shirt complemented his whispering phantom of a mustache and cemented his youthful appearance. Although Luke decided that a good gust of a Santa Ana wind would probably knock him into the street, it was the other guy who irritated him. Luke didn't have the stomach to meet the blond man who was almost certainly Sibyl's date.

"Pleased to meet you," Rex said.

"And this is Marshall Osgood, III, Rex's college roommate," Sibyl chimed in as she nodded towards the fourth member of the dinner party. "Marshall's a stockbroker with Merrill Lynch."

Luke's instant dislike for the six-foot, blond and blue-eyed Marshall cemented when they shook hands. He had the physique of a long distance runner and, in contrast to the Casper Milquetoast version of a handshake offered by Rex, the stockbroker attempted a bone-crusher. It was the premeditated move of someone suffering with an inferiority complex.

Without bothering to reason out why, Luke decided he didn't like the man and responded in kind. His hand dwarfed Sibyl's date's paw and he squeezed just hard enough to make the stockbroker wince and pull his hand back.

He guessed that the stockbroker's expensive clothes constituted an effort to camouflage his lack of masculinity and wondered if Osgood ever bothered to take off his azure colored Yale tie. He couldn't imagine what Sibyl saw in him unless she was trying to please her mother by spending time with someone who'd look good at the family dinner table. Luke felt like a trapped ferret and started strategizing his exit as Sibyl handed him a glass of wine.

"I was just telling everyone about the movie parts I'm up for," Sibyl said.

"Yes, it's really exciting," Rex said. "Her most exciting possibility is a Martin Scorsese film."

Daphne raised her glass. "Here's to Martin Scorsese and to his new star, Sibyl Vane," she said.

"What about the other one?" Rex asked.

"If I get the other one I'll need Luke's help," Sibyl said.

"Me? What could I do to help you?" Judging by the look on Sibyl's date's face, Luke decided that the stockbroker was certain Luke couldn't help Sibyl with anything.

"It's a movie based on Joseph Wambaugh's *The Black Marble*. So I'd need your police expertise." She smiled over her martini glass at Luke.

He had to give her credit. She was really trying to make him comfortable in the awkward situation he'd created.

"Anything I can do," Luke told her.

But the Joseph Wambaugh material obviously held no appeal for the stockbroker who asked, "What's the Scorsese film about?"

"My agent tells me it's about a boxer who ruins his relationships with his wife and brother."

"So would you play the wife?" the stockbroker asked.

"I doubt it. There are a couple other female roles and my agent tells me Scorsese's known for casting unknowns. I certainly fit that category."

"It's all really exciting," Daphne said. "I suspect that soon I'll be selling tickets to people wanting to tour the home where, Sibyl Vane, star of stage and screen used to live."

Luke laughed politely while the others showed their discomfort by laughing a bit too long and too loud.

"Scorsese could really put you in the big time. Are you sure you want to fool around with that cop movie?" the stockbroker asked.

Sibyl's scowl was slight but Luke caught it and he loved her for it. "There's a lot of good cop literature out there and besides, almost any role in a Hollywood production's good for my career."

The stockbroker refused to drop his point. "Well, I'd be careful with the type of movies you choose, let alone the parts you play. Don't do anything cheap."

Luke saw Sibyl's anger rising.

"There's nothing cheap about cops," she said.

Luke decided it was time to leave before his presence was the catalyst for an argument.

"I'll go get another plate for Luke," Daphne said as she headed to the kitchen through swinging café doors.

"No thanks, I can't stay," Luke said. He couldn't stand one more minute in this stifling place and should have figured that a woman like Sibyl would have a date. "I've got to get going. I should have called first."

"Yes, that probably would have been a good idea," the stockbroker said.

Luke nodded and his silence signaled defiance toward the insufferable stock broker. "It was a pleasure to meet you, Daphne, Rex." He scooted for the door and exited as fast as he could.

The drive from Kensington to Point Loma took an agonizing fifteen minutes as Luke mulled over his debacle of an evening. He was sure he and Sibyl had really connected on the ride along especially when they settled down to have dinner. He remembered how her eyes had teared up when he'd talked about losing his mother to cancer. The awkward silence that had accompanied the moment was a bonding experience he'd hoped would never end.

He'd blown it tonight for sure. How stupid was it to show up on her doorstep without calling first?

By the time he pulled into the underground parking area for his apartment complex Denny was already working his shift at Target. At least he could drown his miseries with a couple beers without worrying about Denny getting into any trouble.

He saw the message light as he set his keys onto the kitchen counter. Confident that the message would contain some breathless gushing from one of Denny's bimbos, he hit the play button to clear the machine.

What he heard instead was mildly shocking. "Luke, it's Sibyl. I'm sorry about tonight. Marshall's a total jerk and I sent him home right after you left. Don't go anywhere. I'm coming over to see you."

As the taped voice ended, the phone rang and Luke picked it up.

"Luke? This is Sibyl. I'm so glad I reached you. I need your address. I'm coming over if that's OK."

"Yes, that's OK," Luke said remembering that he'd already told her what neighborhood he and Denny lived in.

"Actually, I'm close. I stopped at a phone booth to double check because I was worried about surprising you."

"I'm here," Luke said.

Luke put Michael Franks' album "The Art of Tea" on the stereo and a bottle of chardonnay in an ice bucket to chill. As he brushed his teeth, his thoughts flashed back to the disco when he'd met Sibyl and felt her body moving against his. The throngs of people surrounding them seemed to disappear as the music played around them.

As he answered the door, Michael Franks' lyrics from Nightmoves filled the room.

*Love is like two dreamers dreamin' the exact same dream*
*Just another Technicolor romance on the screen*

Sibyl tossed her purse onto the couch, picked up the ice bucket and glasses and led Luke into his bedroom.

# 54

LUKE LEFT SIBYL IN THEIR TWISTED SHEETS, slipped into his robe and went to get more wine. A bottle of Beaujolais was the perfect way to celebrate the consummation of their relationship. He knew he was a lucky man as he glanced at the clock and saw that the time was a little past midnight.

After selecting two glasses and opening the wine, he saw the answering machine's blinking light. He'd heard the phone ring several times, but had ignored it. The damn thing could go for days without ever ringing and the one night he had company, the stupid thing wouldn't stop sounding. He couldn't ignore the messages. Denny wasn't home and that stupid sex crimes detail was out there somewhere. As he pushed the button he saw that there were three new messages.

The first was from Shimmer. "Luke I, I'm sorry. I should have known better than to believe what Biletnikoff told me. I'm so stupid. Devree told me you'd been straight with me about Beverly and Hartson and that you'd confronted Hartson about it. I'm not sure how he knew about that, but I believe what he told me. Shit, I'm sorry. I let you down. That asshole Biletnikoff convinced me to give Denny's photos of the councilman's daughter back to him. He said Denny was the beach rapist and you were helping him. I thought-- Never mind what I thought. I was an idiot to believe anything Biletnikoff said. I'm not so hot at saying stuff, am I? I'm just trying to say that I should have known you wouldn't do me wrong.

"You know I cheated on Beverly and I thought that was OK somehow. And then there was the plane crash and then we lost Johnny. Did I ever tell you about Johnny, Luke? What a great kid. He used to go everywhere with me on my days off. Beverly said I was spoiling him but I don't see how that could be true. And then he drowned--"

Shimmer changed the subject after a pause. "Luke, I need help. Call me when you get this. I'm sure I cost Denny his job with the sheriff's office by giving those photos back to Biletnikoff. I cheated on my wife and she cheated on me and everybody cheats on everybody.

"You know that night in the park when I found that old lady? Well, I didn't find her at all. She found me, woke me up in fact. And that's how I broke my hand. She scared the shit out of me and I hit the windshield with my stupid hand and I couldn't tell the truth about that either. I just can't figure out how to help anybody anymore." And then the machine let out a long beep. Shimmer had run out of time.

The next message was from Denny. "Hey Luke, I took the night off and I'm out in Ocean Beach looking for some intensive female therapy. I guess you know that the sheriff's office wouldn't hire me and wouldn't say why. They just said it was something about the background check. I don't get it. Anyway, it's time to party. Later homey."

"Luke, this is Hartson. "Your pal Denny's running around out by the beach and managed to slip away from surveillance somehow. You know him best. If you know where he is, you need to bring him in for questioning. I'm up at Northern. Call me as soon as you get this message."

Hartson picked up on the first ring

"I don't know where Denny is," Luke said.

"Can you find him and bring him in to talk to me?" Hartson asked.

"What do you mean he slipped away from surveillance?" Luke asked.

"He went into a disco down on Grand Avenue somewhere, and nobody could find him after that."

"It's crazy inside those discos," Luke said. "The fact that they couldn't find him doesn't mean anything."

"All I can say is you'd be doing Denny a big favor if you walked him in so I could set up an interview with the guys from sex crimes. I've already got Andee Bradford and Hank Hunter out looking for him and he'd be a lot better off if one of you brought him in."

The doorbell rang while Luke was on the phone. Luke waved Andee Bradford in and asked why Hunter wasn't with her. "He told me his wife called about their daughter being sick so he went home."

"What brings you here this time of night?" Luke asked.

"I'm not sure exactly," Andee answered. "There's something bugging me about Hunter and I thought you might be able to help me sort it out."

"What's going on?" Luke asked.

"I know he seems like the perfect guy and all but Devree knows the backgrounds investigator who hired him. He told Devree some things that are pretty scary. Hunter's real last name is Escobedo. His father was the superintendent of a school district and a deacon at their local church until he was convicted of raping and murdering his wife. He repeatedly raped her at gunpoint and made Hunter watch. As soon as Hank was old enough, he changed his name to Hunter, looking for a new start.

"Every Saturday, there were family work details to keep the home looking perfect and if any of the kids didn't do their part, Dad made Hank tie their hands up with duct tape and put a gag in their mouths. His mother stood by while her kids were terrorized and didn't call the cops when Dad raped her. Hank finally did call and was the main witness at the trial before he finished high school. His life has been a total wreck, yet he manages to always say the right things and be at the right places all the time, like when he implicated Denny in the rape series. You and I both know that's total crap but its turned Hunter into a hero somehow."

The sound of Andee's words dropped on Luke's ears with the impact of a bomb exploding in a confined space. "He told me he wasn't at lineup when Denny's name first came up," Luke said.

"All I can tell you is that Chief Browner specifically said Hunter had told Sergeant Hartson that Denny might be the rapist, which is why the Sarge alerted Sex Crimes."

Luke's swallow came hard like he was gagging down a spoonful of sand. Everything was finally starting to make sense. Hunter had been at their apartment the night he joined Luke and Denny at Crystal T's Emporium. He'd used the restroom in Denny's room then taken his jacket to the trunk of his car. Now Denny's flashlight was missing and the rapist always blinded his victims with a flashlight. At the scene of the plane crash, Hunter's eyes looked dead, just the way the empty eye sockets had looked on the skull at the Pickwick Hotel. Denny and Hunter were both of Black and Hispanic descent and of similar height and weight but everyone who heard the theory that the rapist was either a current or a former cop wanted to believe he had to be a disgraced former cop, not someone still working the streets.

"Who followed Denny tonight?" Luke asked.

"Hunter and me," Andee said. "I went into a 7-11 for a cup of coffee and to make a phone call and when I caught up with him, Hunter told me Denny had gone into a bar. I went inside to look for him while Hunter waited outside and Denny wasn't there."

"It's him," Luke said.

"Who's what?"

"Hunter's the rapist. I don't have time to go into it now, but I'm sure it's Hunter. He knows that everyone on the detail is actively looking for Denny. He knows where the surveillances are set up and he's taken the night off. He intends to strike tonight."

Luke saw the light of recognition click in Andee's eyes. "I'm going looking for Hunter," he told her. "You look for Denny inside the discos in Pacific Beach and get him some place safe."

Luke gave Andee the number to Hartson's desk at Northern Division, asked her to fill him in and warned her not to tell anyone else. "Hunter's the department's golden boy of the moment and nobody'll believe he's the rapist until we prove it to them," he said.

Luke rushed into the bedroom to get dressed and didn't have time to give Sibyl a decent explanation other than that he had to leave to handle an emergency.

# 55

A SLIVER MOON SPLASHED A SMIDGEN OF LIGHT ONTO the waves and sand of Moonlight Beach in Encinitas, several miles north of La Jolla Shores. Luke hugged the edge of a bar of jutting rocks, scouring the area for Hunter or a young couple. He'd decided on this location after turning the crime data over in his head as he drove and had found Hunter's car a couple blocks away. Hunter was clever, knew how cops thought and had managed to avoid leaving a clear pattern of location and day of the week. But Luke was convinced that once the sex crimes investigators looked into it, they'd learn that Hunter's wife was away on overnight trips when the rapes occurred. Hunter had told him that the sex crimes detail was concentrating on the southerly beaches and had made a point of convincing them that Denny was lurking in the Pacific Beach area. Luke had hoped that Hunter would return to the scene of his original rape and was lucky enough to be right. Even with Denny hobbled like a scapegoat, the tightrope was squeezing Hunter's neck and he had to know he couldn't avoid detection much longer. Tonight might be the last time before he got caught and the lure of the original rape scene could allow him to recreate the original euphoric high.

He hunkered down in a cleft of the rocks with a clear view of the beach and soon spied a couple hugging in ostentatious foreplay as they walked in tandem about midway between the waterline and the parking lot. They soon disappeared from sight and Luke climbed atop the rocks to keep them in sight. That's when a wiry man wearing a ski mask and black gloves emerged from the shadows. He carried a flashlight, wore a coiled rope wrapped around his neck and walked in a path that would intercept the couple in a secluded area.

As he crouched on the rocks, Luke started to get a handle on Hunter's thoughts. He remembered the almost palpable disgust on Hunter's face for the woman at the domestic violence call whose only fault was fear of her husband. Now he intended to ravage two lives simply because they'd chosen seclusion on a public beach. By forcing the woman to tie her man up and then making him watch, Hunter would destroy their ability to trust for the rest of their lives.

Luke eased down from the rocks and tried to keep concealed so Hunter couldn't spot him right away. The only way to stop Hunter was to catch him in the act.

His head pounded as he ran toward the stalking rapist who confronted the couple with a gun and flashed a light in the man's eyes. Although it was difficult to see as Luke ran in the near darkness, Hunter held the flashlight away from his body the way Hartson had said he would and even managed to do it as he grabbed the woman's hair and threw her to the sand. This had to be a perfect moment for Hunter who intended to rape the woman, humiliate the man and prove how stupid they both were to be on the beach at night. It had to be a sweet irony for him to prove how wrong they were in their complacency.

Closer now, Luke was able to hear what the three were saying.

"Tie him up." Hunter thrust the rope into the woman's hands. "You'll both die if he gets loose."

He shoved his gun toward the woman's face and ordered her to pick up the rope when it dropped into the sand. She started to cry. When she couldn't muster the courage to move, he picked up the rope and strode toward the man, who lunged at him. As the two grappled, the gun exploded, a bullet kicking up sand between them. Hunter hit the man a glancing blow to the head with the flashlight. As the victim fell, he pulled Hunter on top of him and the gun went off before Hunter started tying the man's hands behind him.

Luke emerged from the shadows, knocked Hunter to the ground and the gun went flying. It landed a foot or so away.

The two police officers lunged for the gun. Hunter snatched it up. Luke pushed it away from his body, his nails digging into Hunter's arm as they fought over control of the firearm.

Hunter started pulling his hand free but the woman mustered courage to clutch a fist full of sand and throw it into his eyes. When Hunter reached up to wipe the sand away, Luke picked him up and drove him backward. They fell over the gunshot victim who'd managed to crawl forward trying to help. The gun went off as they fell. A bullet pierced Luke's hand, but he kept fighting, helped by the young couple who'd been helpless moments before.

The ski mask fell to the sand as the woman scratched at Hunter's eyes. Her wounded partner repeatedly kicked the rapist in the side of the head. There were no helpless victims here, only an angry trio of people fighting against the barbaric attack of a man bent on destroying their lives.

Hunter had come here to pull the woman's pants down and enter her while her trussed up man watched. Instead, the woman nearly scratched out his eyes while the wounded man kicked him in the head. The gun fired again. A bullet tore through Hunter's shoulder. He pulled away from the tangle and ran for the parking lot as his three victims lay exhausted in the sand.

Tonight, Luke was a victim too who lay in the sand gathering his wits until he remembered that the man lying near him had been shot. He rolled to his side and sat up to see the woman bending over her man.

"He needs to get to a hospital," the woman said. "And so do you."

"Can he walk?" Luke asked.

She shook her head. "I don't think so."

"My car's nearby." Luke bent and slung the wounded man's arm over his shoulder. He started dragging him toward his car with the woman trotting alongside.

"Who are you and where did you come from?" the woman asked.

"My name's Luke and I'm a police officer who was passing by," Luke said.

She looked at the hand Luke was using to support her friend's weight. "You're bleeding," she said. "What can I do to help?"

"You can drive us to the hospital. Here's my car," Luke said.

Luke used his good hand to shove the man into the back seat then climbed in next to him. "What are your names?" Luke asked.

"I'm Diane and this is Roger."

"Do you know how to get to Scripps Green Hospital, Diane?"

She nodded as Luke put Roger's head in his lap.

# 56

DIANE PULLED LUKE'S MERCURY TRACER INTO THE ambulance bay at
the hospital, threw it in park and went running into the emergency room.
She ran out moments later with two medical people pushing a gurney
and a third pushing a wheelchair. They laid Roger on the gurney and
hustled him inside. Luke was pushed along in the chair behind them.

Luke stood as soon as he was inside and called Sergeant Hartson's
desk at northern. "Sarge, Hunter shot me and I shot him. I'm in the
Urgent Care at Green," Luke said.

"Where's Hunter?" Hartson asked.

"He ran. I have no idea where he went. There's another gunshot victim here with me at the hospital and you'd better send somebody up to
Moonlight Beach in Encinitas right away to secure the scene and look
for evidence."

Luke did his best to describe the location of the crime scene before
one of the doctors made him hang up the phone and took him into an
exam room to treat his hand.

When Hartson hurried in a few minutes later his radio came to life
with the dispatcher directing him to the hospital across the freeway a
short distance from them. "Respond to a 245 shooting. The victim's at
Scripps Memorial and the medical staff have identified him as a former
police officer by the name of Denny Durango."

Hartson shook his head in disbelief. "What makes you so certain the other victim is Hunter?" Hartson asked.

"I fought with him, Sarge, with a lot of help from his two other victims. She managed to pull off his ski mask. It's Hunter all right."

"Why would they say it's Durango?"

"Fuck, Sarge. How would I know?" Luke shouted. "But I know who it is and if you get somebody over to the other hospital, you'll know too."

Luke's injury turned out to be mostly superficial. The bullet had passed through the fleshy part of his palm below the pinkie finger. The doctor cleaned and disinfected the wound, bandaged it and delivered a quick lecture on proper aftercare. Luke refused an injection for pain but accepted the doctor's prescription for later.

Hartson checked on the other victims. Roger had lost a lot of blood but would recover. Diane had twisted her ankle in the fight but was otherwise fine.

When Luke started to leave, Hartson told him he needed to wait for someone from Internal Affairs who was on the way to interview him.

"I need to go," Luke told him. "It'll have to wait."

"I'm ordering you to stay here until this all gets sorted out," Hartson said.

Given that Hartson was betraying Shimmer, Luke was reluctant to confide in him, but he knew he had no other choice. "I'm worried about Shimmer," he said.

"What's he done now?" Hartson asked.

"He left me a phone message." Luke paused. "He sounded scary, talking about Johnny and losing Beverly to you."

"When was this?"

"His message came through before the one you left for me."

"That was hours ago," Hartson said. "We'd better hurry."

# 57

SLEEP HAD ONCE AGAIN ELUDED J. R. SHIMMER. The Jack Daniels didn't quiet his nerves and the pain in his hand had ratcheted up to maximum velocity. He took another big swig, closed his eyes and saw Mrs. Turnbow as her husband nearly cut her head off. If only he could have saved her life. Things might be different now somehow.

He couldn't stop the moving pictures in his head or the soundtrack in his ears. Mrs. Turnbow had never really spoken but in Shimmer's version she cried out, "Please don't let him kill me." It didn't matter that he'd killed her husband. She was still dead. He saw a trail of scarlet blood trailing away from her body as she lay on the floor. Her husband's blood intermixed with hers and oozed toward the kitchen.

He couldn't save Johnny either and he couldn't save Beverly and he was only alive because of Luke Jones. He used to tell Beverly everything but he couldn't talk to her anymore. He couldn't talk to anyone really. He was like a patient on an operating table whose anesthesia hadn't worked properly. He could hear and see everybody and everything but nobody could see or hear him.

Then there was the old lady in the park. His broken hand was a constant reminder of her. Talk about not being able to speak. He couldn't tell anyone the truth about that and Biletnikoff had given him a commendation and called him a hero. Some hero. If the woman hadn't fallen on his squad car she'd be dead in the park right now.

He'd lost Beverly because he couldn't forgive her for letting Johnny drown. She didn't even exist for him anymore. Every time he looked at her, he saw Johnny. Then he'd suck in a little air and try to remember how to breathe, forgetting that she couldn't breathe either. It was his job to help her but he couldn't, because he was too deep in the fog of his own misery.

Then she took up with Hartson and now she was moving in with him and her words echoed in Shimmer's head. "He reminds me of you before you hated me."

Shimmer poured another generous slug of Jack Daniels and raised his glass in a toast. "Here's to your happiness Beverly. And may T.D. Hartson rot in hell."

As the whiskey's numbing qualities trickled down his throat, he remembered faithless friends. He was first in line when it came to them and should probably give Hartson a break for betraying him. After all, he'd let Biletnikoff manipulate him into screwing over the guy who'd saved his life.

Luke was a great guy and a good friend and he was sorry he'd misjudged him. Luke had saved his life then accepted him as a friend. Shimmer still believed that arrogant rookies should be put in their place. But Luke was different somehow. Luke was OK. It was Shimmer who was the false friend. He should've believed Luke when he said Denny couldn't be the rapist.

He'd called Luke earlier and left him a message but wasn't surprised that Luke hadn't called him back. Shimmer'd delivered the Tina Cleveland pictures back to Biletnikoff who'd used them to prevent Denny from being hired. And Luke had to know that.

Shimmer's thoughts summed up his life. He was a failed hero, a false friend, a faithless husband and husband to a faithless wife.

# 58

"I'M COMING WITH YOU," HARTSON SAID. The tone in his voice signaled an end to any argument.

Luke was disgusted that Hartson hadn't considered Shimmer's importance instead of taking up with Beverly in the first place. But what good would it do to tell him that?

The two men drove in silence until Hartson slowed the police car in front of Shimmer's house. Luke opened his door before the vehicle stopped moving. He unfolded himself from the car as the radio sounded.

They hurried toward the front door with its paint peeling away at the edges. The weeds had already won their battle against the lawn. The bushes swallowed up most of the walkway and the concrete stoop of the porch had broken away in chunks at the edges.

A silhouette appeared at the window. The shadowy figure raised a glass to its lips. Luke told Hartson that Shimmer was OK but then Hartson's radio sounded from the scene of the attempted rape.

"Sarge, I've found a P.D. flashlight here on the beach. The name etched on it is D. Durango who I believe used to be with the P.D."

As those words hung in the air, a second officer calling from Scripps Memorial asked Hartson to switch to the tactical frequency. "Here's the thing, Sarge," the officer said. "I saw this gunshot victim being wheeled into the operating room and it's not Durango, it's Hank Hunter."

Luke felt a weight lift from his shoulders. This whole thing was Hartson's problem now.

"What's his status?" Hartson asked.

"He's unconscious and has lost a lot of blood, but I'm told he'll recover."

"That bastard tried to kill me and ruin Denny's life," Luke said.

"I'll be coming to the hospital in a little while," Hartson said. "In the meantime, you can expect visits from folks from Homicide and Internal Affairs."

"OK, Sarge. Are you enroute now?" the officer asked.

"Negative, but I will be in a few minutes."

Luke had helped catch the bad guy and had proven that Denny wasn't the rapist. Shimmer was OK. He was just on the other side of the door, and things were starting to look good.

Luke knocked on the door.

Instead of the door swinging open to greet them, the sound of a gunshot came from inside then something toppled to the floor.

# 59

Lieutenant Rood, papers in hand, walked into Chief Coleman's outer office and shined a smile at his secretary. "Hi Donna, how are you?"

Donna returned the smile. "Can't complain."

The Chief's door was open. "May I?" she asked.

"He's expecting you," Donna said.

Coleman nodded as Rood placed the papers she'd been carrying on his desk.

The Chief picked up the stack. After he'd read for a moment he looked up and raised a questioning eyebrow. "This is the original evaluation Biletnikoff submitted on Officer Jones?"

Caroline Rood nodded.

"One more nail," he said. "And am I correct in thinking this was submitted before Jones captured Officer Hunter over the weekend?"

"Yes."

"So these pinheads wanted to go after the cop who's been a hero in the past few months more times than I can count?"

Lieutenant Rood nodded and shifted in her chair. "I've been reviewing Hunter's record. His childhood was a total nightmare and his father's in prison for killing his mother. But Hunter insists that his parents died in the PSA plane crash and that he saw them holding hands."

Coleman lit a cigarette. "That plane crash destroyed a lot of lives," he said. Then he took a puff and blew smoke into the air.

"I've reviewed J.R. Shimmer's records as well," Rood said. "His wife was leaving him to move in with Sgt. Hartson. His son drowned. Of course you remember the debacle with the man who killed his wife in front of him. To be frank, I'm surprised he lasted as long as he did and I'm betting that phony commendation he received played into his suicide somehow. What could Browner possibly hope to accomplish by giving out special recognition for finding the old lady? The other officer on the scene, Fiedler, said the whole situation smelled bad from the moment he arrived. Browner had to have been working some angle."

Coleman picked up another sheet of paper and gave it a slight wave. "Biletnikoff worked the crash too. I'm hoping I can use that and the suicide of one of his men to order him in for counseling." Coleman shook his head. "Do you believe this anonymous note saying that he was the one who urinated on your desk?"

"Yes sir, I do."

Coleman puffed harder on his cigarette. "Without the author coming forward, I can't use it formally. I can't believe that Browner wants to promote such an unstable man but I'm sure it has to do with Biletnikoff's doing his dirty work."

Coleman put his cigarette out and lit another one. "You'd better get going," he said. "My meeting with Browner starts in a few minutes and the less he knows about your involvement in all this, the better. Good work and thanks," Coleman said.

Caroline Rood smiled and left.

# 60

CHIEF COLEMAN FIGURED THAT LT. ROOD HAD narrowly cleared the corridor before Browner appeared in his outer office. From what he heard, Browner forewent his usual banter with Donna. Coleman checked his watch. Donna's instructions were to keep Browner waiting for five minutes. Coleman wanted his subordinate properly tenderized before their meeting started.

Donna rang through to him a few minutes later and Coleman told her to send Browner in. His deputy needed to be reminded who the real chief was. Coleman stayed seated behind his desk, looking at the stack of papers in his hand. When he finally looked up, he left Browner standing.

"I think you'll remember that we had a meeting not too long ago where I warned you not to mess with any of my people," Coleman said in a quiet voice.

He picked up the first file. "This is you messing with my people." He took the next file off the stack. "And this is you messing with my people too. Your handprints are all over this ridiculous evaluation of Luke Jones." Coleman waved the original evaluation then picked up a second report. "This is the corrected version that continues to rate him as a superior officer."

"That guy disobeys orders and he should--"

Coleman cut him off, "You'd better keep your mouth shut. I'm just getting started. I'll get back to Jones in a minute after you've explained that commendation you presented to Officer Shimmer for just barely doing his job. What did you think you could accomplish?"

"He found that old lady who was in danger and I thought it would help counteract the bad press the beach rapist was giving us," Browner said.

Coleman clucked his tongue. "It seems to me your efforts would have been better directed at finding the rotten apple than currying favor with the press. Besides, it's time you learned that dealing with the press is in my purview, not yours."

"That's the thanks I get for trying to help." Browner's voice lacked conviction.

Coleman could have lost his temper if he weren't so clearly standing on a mountain of victory.

"Help? Don't you believe that an officer should have to perform extraordinarily to deserve an award? Stumbling across some old lady doesn't cut it in my book. You probably helped push that poor officer over the edge."

"You're accusing me of being complicit in his suicide? That's too much!" Browner shouted.

Things were looking up. Coleman had a distinct edge when Browner lost his temper. "I think you and your phony award factored into his misery but let's move on to the next point. I want you to order your pet sergeant into counseling."

Browner's rage threatened to push him over the edge of control. "He's not my pet and he's as right as rain. What are you talking about?"

"He pissed all over Lt. Rood's desk. Do you call that being 'right as rain'?" Coleman shot back.

Browner's confused expression convinced Coleman that he knew nothing of the desk peeing incident. He supposed the good news was that Biletnikoff had thought that particular stunt up all by himself.

"You get him into counseling or I'll see that he loses his job."

"Is that it?" Browner demanded. "Or can we move on to that alleged hero Luke Jones?"

"I've only met Officer Jones once but I've reviewed his file. He was an outstanding recruit and is turning into a solid officer and you'd better keep your hands off him. What I can't understand is what you have against him. It's not like he'll challenge you for your job any time soon."

"He's a punk rookie who talks back to his superiors, supports that idiot Denny Durango and disobeyed orders when he went to Moonlight Beach Saturday night but then he got lucky and caught the guy."

Coleman picked up a different file, opened it and leafed through it. "I see, like he got lucky spotting those cop-killing bank robbers from L.A.? Or how he got lucky when he saved Shimmer's life? If that's luck then I want about a hundred more lucky guys just like him."

Coleman picked up the original employee evaluation that had rated Luke as a deficient officer. "What were you angling for with this?" he asked.

Browner ignored the question. "He still disobeyed orders. You can't expect to run a department efficiently when you've got officers who do that."

"I agree, which is why I called you in here. You've been disobeying my orders and it had better stop right now."

"Don't make this about me," Browner said. "Jones wasn't supposed to be anywhere near that beach and you know it."

"I don't know any such thing," Coleman said. "In fact, I know just the opposite." The puzzled look that settled over Browner's features was worth waiting for. "Luke Jones was acting directly according to my orders."

Browner sat back in his seat and turned pale. Coleman thought he must be wishing for a banana or a granola bar about now. He shook a cigarette out of its pack, lit up and blew the smoke towards Browner.

"There are consequences for getting in my way, Hal. I haven't decided what they are yet, but you need to be certain that I will penalize you."

# 61

THE GROWING CROWD PUSHED LUKE ON TOP of the bar in the One-Five-three Club and he surveyed their up-turned faces. His audience was usually comprised mostly of peers and a few mid-level superiors who took distinct sides in their appraisal of Luke Jones. He was hated and respected in almost equal numbers. But this occasion was different than most.

His audience had all just left Shimmer's funeral and tonight he wanted to talk about his dead friend. No matter what any of his audience thought of him or of J.R. Shimmer, they all dreaded cop suicide and were here to honor the memory of one of their own.

He surveyed the faces below him and wondered if the pain that reflected on their faces showed on his own. Andee Bradford stood in a group with Caroline Rood, Paul Devree, Bob Fiedler and several of the dispatchers. Dick Arenas and Constantin Biletnikoff stood with their usual group of rookie baiters, but Luke didn't have the mental energy to summon his usual dose of animosity toward them.

Luke saw Nine-John-Randolph standing with Denny in front of Chief Coleman and Beverly Shimmer and Hartson were near the rear. Nadine Brown, otherwise known as Mrs. 'Yat was there, and she nodded slightly at Luke when their eyes met.

Sibyl Vane gave him an encouraging smile.

As he opened his mouth to speak, Luke considered the lives of one former friend who'd turned into a serial rapist and a former foe turned friend who'd ended his life by sticking a loaded pistol to his temple.

Hunter, who'd changed his name in shame and had fooled others into thinking he'd had everything to live for, would spend the rest of his life in prison. As with so many families, the Escobedo bunch seemingly had everything going for them, access to the best colleges and a sled ride to wealth, power and happiness. But how could a helpless child who grew up to become a great athlete reconcile himself to watching his mother being repeatedly raped at gunpoint by her husband? Hank Hunter could offer no excuses for what he'd done but, surely some understanding had to come with the knowledge of his childhood circumstances.

Luke wanted to drive his anger and hatred toward Hunter out of his body. The man had disgraced them all while conniving to make Denny take the fall and had cost Denny his chance at a job with the Sheriff's Office. He had lied to everyone. Luke understood the ravages of a crappy childhood but how could Hunter allow his past to abrogate his seemingly perfect future?

J.R. Shimmer had less ostentatious possibilities in store for him than Hunter would have. But he mostly tried to be honorable and looked out for the weak and the helpless to keep them safe. How could a simple man like him make his way in the world when he couldn't save a woman's life by killing her husband?

When Luke had finally reached home on the night of Shimmer's death, the answering machine's red light was flashing on and off. Luke thought Sibyl must have left him a message. But the voice had belonged instead to Shimmer, and he heard the words repeating in his head. "I can't believe you brought Hartson with you. Seeing him is the last straw. I'm done. Please look in on Mrs. 'Yat. Thanks for being my friend, Luke. I'm sorry. Goodbye." No gunshot was recorded. Shimmer had hung up before he fired the shot that ended his life.

Luke wanted to speak without tears but he wasn't sure it was possible. He thought about the first time he had quoted Shakespeare at the One-Five-Three Club and how Shimmer had kept demanding to know,

"What'd he say?" But the last time he quoted Shakespeare on the bar it was Shimmer who instigated it and kept demanding more. Luke had disliked the little guy at first but he'd come to respect and value him as a friend. He knew that Shimmer would've demanded that he quote something from the Bard and Luke wanted to do right by his friend.

Was Bardolph the right character to quote? After all Shimmer wanted to be with Johnny "wheresome'er he is, either in heaven or in hell!" But no one would believe that a three year old went anywhere but to heaven.

Luke swallowed and told the story of Mrs. 'Yat and how Shimmer had befriended and protected her even though he failed at saving others and ultimately couldn't save himself. And then Luke found the right words from Shakespeare for his friend, "To be, or not to be, that is the question…" But his mind quickly slipped away from the text as he contemplated what the words actually meant. Hamlet was asking if it might be better to commit suicide than suffer the ravages of living an unfair life. But it was more than that too. It was a speech about the meaning of life, a question about whether it might be better never to have lived at all. Luke suspected that Shimmer would have come down on the side of eternal oblivion but that would have deprived a lot of people of their association with a good man who did his best to help others.

# Acknowledgments

SPECIAL THANKS GO OUT TO LINDA A. SHUBECK WHO volunteered to help the author as he recovered from a serious surgery and struggled with his commitment to meet the book's deadline. It's safe to say that this book could not have been written without her partnership and friendship.

Thanks also to Jean Jenkins whose editorial eye polished the manuscript and to Barry Kraft who added his Shakespearean expertise to the editorial process and his mellifluous voice to the audiobook version.

# About the Author

T.B. SMITH SERVED AS A POLICE OFFICER FOR twenty-seven years with the City of San Diego and San Diego Unified School District Police Departments, retiring as a lieutenant in 2003, after being injured in an on-duty traffic accident. He's a graduate of San Diego State University, where he studied English Literature and creative writing. He is the author of *The Sticking Place*, the first novel in the Luke Jones series. He currently lives in Ashland, Oregon, where he enjoys attending the Oregon Shakespeare Festival.